Mary Bennet

Mary Bennet

A Novella
in the
Personages of *Pride & Prejudice Collection*

JENNIFER BECTON

A WHITELEY PRESS, LLC, BOOK

A WHITELEY PRESS, LLC, BOOK

Copyright © 2014 by Jennifer Becton
http://www.bectonliterary.com
14   2 3 4 5 6 7

ISBN-13: 978-0-9908725-0-4
ISBN-10: 0990872505

Cover: Cover: Edmund Blair Leighton, *Singing to the Reverend.* (Image in public domain.)

The characters and events in this book are fictitious or used fictitiously. Any similarity to real people, living or dead, is coincidental and not intended by the author.

OTHER WORKS BY JENNIFER BECTON

THE PERSONAGES OF *PRIDE & PREJUDICE* COLLECTION
Charlotte Collins
Caroline Bingley
"Maria Lucas": A Short Story
The Personages of Pride & Prejudice *Collection*

⁓ ❦ ⁓

THE SOUTHERN FRAUD THRILLER SERIES
Writing as J. W. Becton

Absolute Liability
Death Benefits
At Fault
Moral Hazard
Shock Loss—Coming Soon

⁓ ❦ ⁓

∞∞ ∞∞

[Jane Austen] would, if asked, tell us many little particulars about the
subsequent career of some of her people.
In this traditionary way, we learned that…
Mary [Bennet]…was content to be considered a star in the society of
Meriton [sic].

∞∞ James Austen Leigh, *Memoir of Jane Austen* ∞∞

∞∞ ∞∞

๑๑ One ๑๑

1813

"Come along, Mary!" Mrs. Bennet trilled in a tone that sent shivers up the backs of every resident of Longbourn.

Above stairs, Mary jolted upright in her chair and dropped the weighty tome she had been reading, causing it to crash to the floorboards with a resounding thud.

"Good heavens!" Mrs. Bennet cried with increased shrillness. "What was that? Do not tell me that you have tripped and torn your morning gown, clumsy child. And just when we have an important call to pay."

"I dropped my book, nothing more, Mama," Mary called as she heaved the text from the floor and carefully placed it on the little writing table beside her.

"What did you say? Well, one torn garment here or there is no matter to me. The Bennets are no longer paupers thanks to the fortuitous marriages of your elder sisters. We can afford a new gown for you. Perhaps I shall have one myself!"

Mrs. Bennet's soliloquy paused, and then she added more loudly, "Oh! The hour is later than I anticipated. Pick yourself up, Mary. We must be off even now if we are to arrive at your Aunt Philips's house to greet the new young lady."

Mary obediently appeared at the head of the stairs, prepared for the usual commentary on her appearance and the inevitable comparison to one of her *beautiful* sisters.

But neither came.

Instead, her mother took her in from coiffure to boots.

"I see you did not damage your gown. Good for you, my dear. Now do come along."

Pleasure rippled through Mary at her mother's response, for it was as near to matronly approval as she ever received. Having four sisters, all of whom shone with beauty, talent, wit, and vivacity, plain Mary had all but disappeared amidst the fray.

Now, with three sisters married and her younger sister Kitty gone to stay at Pemberley, Mary was the only daughter who remained at home. Finally, she had the opportunity to shine.

Smiling at her mother, Mary trod down the stairs, donned her pelisse and bonnet, and hurried to the waiting carriage.

Meryton lay one mile distant from Longbourn, but even in such fine spring weather, Mrs. Bennet preferred to travel there by carriage. Mary, who despised walking, looked with gratitude upon her mother's preference.

"Arriving at one's destination in a carriage is far more dignified than doing so on foot," Mary mused, her eyes focused on the passing countryside.

"Oh, for heaven's sake, Mary," Mrs. Bennet said, sighing heavily. "Do not moralize the morning away, and certainly not while we form a new acquaintance."

Mary frowned. "Moralize? What do you mean, Mama?"

"Do not be difficult, child." Mrs. Bennet rolled her eyes. "You know how off-putting your musings over principles and literature can become."

Embarrassed and confused, Mary felt her cheeks reddened. She leaned forward in her seat, her brown eyes imploring even as her fingers tightened reflexively in the fabric of her skirt.

"You do not approve of my conversation?" she squeaked. "I have always made proper conversation a particular focus of study."

"And you should have learned that displaying too much knowledge does you no credit."

Mary knew the maxims well, and she recited them for her mother. "A young lady must be educated enough to speak skillfully on any subject, though she must also deliver the words with a certain humility and feminine reserve. I am nothing if not humble and reserved, Mama."

"Do not be obtuse," her mother said, frustrated. "No one wants to hear moral lessons over a nice meal, no matter how humble you sound. Morality is bad for the digestion."

Mary's eyes narrowed as she considered her mother's reply. An attitude such as that was surely to blame for her youngest sister's disastrous matrimonial choices. Unrestrained emotions and a lack of parental correction had resulted in poor Lydia's downfall.

Mary chose not to mention this truth to her mother, who refused to think ill of her youngest child.

Mistaking Mary's silence as a cue to impart a valuable lesson, Mrs. Bennet focused her attention on her daughter. "You must do as I do, Mary, and *listen* attentively to your companions. Do not plan your next comment while others speak."

Mary grimaced at the flaw in her mother's reasoning. "But, Mama, how will I know what to say if I am not allowed to ponder my words beforehand?"

Mrs. Bennet threw up her hands. "Conversations must not always be fraught with meaning. Forget your sermons and quotations, and discuss something pretty, like the weather."

Disappointment lanced Mary at the thought of being confined to trivial subjects. She leaned back and turned to peer out the coach's window.

Mary did not excel at chitchat. She never knew what to say in response to "pretty" topics. How many times must a group of women comment on the fine weather or the state of the roads?

She likewise despised conversations in which she was required to render her own opinions extemporaneously. Her thoughts seemed to freeze, and she could not think of how to respond. If she did manage to form her words into sentences, she inevitably committed a verbal *faux pas*. Therefore, she had come to lean heavily on the thoughts of great writers and would draw them from her memory as the conversation required.

But this, to her mother, constituted moralizing. Mary simply could not comprehend it. She faced her mother again.

"I believed the discussion of books to be an appropriate topic for a woman of sense and education. I only—"

"I am ever so anxious to make the acquaintance of the sister of your uncle's new clerk," Mrs. Bennet interrupted, her mind already committed to the next topic. "The young lady in particular is said to be the epitome of kindness and affability, and your uncle is quite impressed by his new clerk. I hope that you shall not give offense upon this meeting, Mary, for it may prove more important that you realize."

Upon her mother's ominous words, fear skittered up Mary's spine, and her palms began to sweat. She wiped them on her already wrinkled skirt.

"What do you mean?" she asked, trying to read her mother's intentions from her facial expression. "Why is this meeting so important?"

Mrs. Bennet grinned slyly. "Never you mind that, Mary. I had not the least notion of causing you apprehension. You know I never intend to put pressure on my children. Just mind that you remain on your best behavior."

Mrs. Bennet had a secret, and that alone would have been sufficient to make Mary feel uneasy, but now she was also unsure of the very basics of social intercourse. She risked embarrassing herself and shaming her mother in a situation for which it was impossible to prepare. Her mother left her no opportunity to plan or readjust.

Mary hoped that her mother might realize her daughter's predicament and offer more detailed advice, but Mrs. Bennet merely prattled on about the antics of some neighbor or other, leaving Mary to draw the only conclusion she could.

This mysterious meeting was doomed to failure before it ever occurred.

✣ Two ✣

Mrs. Philips laid aside her mending the moment Mary and Mrs. Bennet entered her small, liberally furnished sitting room.

"Oh, Sister," wailed Mrs. Bennet as she charged forward, narrowly avoiding collisions with two small tables and a sofa. "Have we missed her? I warned Mary that if she did not hurry, the young lady would have come and gone before we ever stepped foot from Longbourn."

Mrs. Philips shook her head at Mrs. Bennet's theatrics. "There is no need for panic, I assure you. Miss Hardcastle has not yet paid her call."

Mrs. Bennet flopped onto a nearby sofa, dislodging at least three cushions in the process. Mary took the adjacent seat, lowering herself in a much more careful manner.

"Good morning, Aunt Philips," Mary said, readjusting the cushions around her.

"It is a lovely morning, is it not?" her aunt replied, waving a hand at the brave streak of sunlight that peeked through her excessively ornate draperies. "I do hope your introduction to the Hardcastle siblings will render it even brighter."

Mary blinked rapidly. She sucked in a few quick breaths, leaving her slightly lightheaded.

"The Hardcastle *siblings*?" she blurted.

"Why, yes." Mrs. Philips looked puzzled. "Miss Hardcastle and her brother, Mr. Hardcastle."

Now Mary understood why her mother deemed this meeting so important. "I am to be introduced to a gentleman?" she demanded.

The two older women sat in silence, shocked at Mary's uncharacteristic outburst.

Taking a slower, deeper breath, Mary attempted to recover her composure. She shifted in her seat and spoke with great deliberation. "I was given to understand that Miss Hardcastle *alone* would be calling."

"Oh no!" her aunt exclaimed. "Mr. Philips vowed that Mr. Hardcastle too would call upon us, and he will make the necessary introduction. Is that not kind of him?"

Upon this announcement, Mary felt the opposite of pleasure. Her eyes darted to her mother, who regarded her with a mixture of delight and expectation. Mary could not return her mother's beaming smile, for she comprehended the situation with terrible clarity. This was far from an innocent morning call to meet a new young lady. This was a matchmaking arrangement of the least subtle variety.

She could not afford to fall prey to her unstable emotions. She must compose herself.

Mary momentarily closed her eyes, and when she opened them, she managed to say, "It is very kind of my uncle."

Mrs. Philips exchanged a glance with Mrs. Bennet and then returned her attention to Mary. "You must be quite lonely now that your sisters have all married or gone from home."

Mary opened her mouth to respond, but her mother was faster.

"Mary could never be lonely. Oh no! We have been in each other's company constantly, and we have so much to occupy our time. During the day, we go to the milliner or the dressmaker, and in the evenings, Mary reads to me, though I do not always approve of her choice of material. What is so awful about novels? She says she will not read them, but I do so prefer a dashing hero over her axioms and parables. I shall break her of sermon-reading, for no one wants to hear sermons…not even in church!"

Before Mrs. Bennet could leap to yet another subject, a knock sounded at the door.

Mary jolted and spun in her seat. She licked her suddenly parched lips and wondered how she would ever survive the morning.

"Oh!" Mrs. Bennet cried, sitting upright and adjusting her gown. "Your posture, Mary! Do sit up straight, and remember what I said in the carriage. We will have none of your morbid musings today!"

Mary stiffened her spine and wished she might disappear beneath the rug before the guests entered. But that was not to be.

Instead, the servant swung open the door and announced Miss Hardcastle.

Mary's lips dropped open. Rather than feeling relief that Mr. Hardcastle was not at the door, she experienced only horror.

Miss Hardcastle was the stuff of which nightmares are composed: curling blonde hair, wide blue eyes, and a willowy figure. Though Mary could hardly claim fashion expertise, she could see very well that Miss Hardcastle took care with her wardrobe. Her cornflower blue dress—though modest and unadorned—flattered her figure and coloring.

This young lady's beauty far surpassed even her sister Jane's.

Mary stood, quickly assessing her own appearance. She wore a muted green dress and sturdy boots, and her straight hair was done up simply. Compared to Miss Hardcastle, she might as well have been another piece of upholstered furniture that littered the room.

This was the woman her mother wanted her to befriend? This beauty? Why must Mary always be outshone by her companions?

"Allow me to present Miss Hardcastle," Mrs. Philips said, sending forward her charge. The young woman stepped gracefully through the narrow space allowed by the older woman's abundant furnishings and beamed at Mary.

Mary forced herself to smile in return as they exchanged curtsies.

"I am ever so pleased to make your acquaintance, Miss Bennet," Miss Hardcastle said, her voice soft and kind.

Though Miss Hardcastle's reserved tone eased Mary's nerves, she felt great paranoia over misspeaking.

"Thank you. I am ever so pleased to make *your* acquaintance...too."

Mary blushed at her obvious parroting. Anyone who heard her must think her a simpleton. She must say something to assure Miss Hardcastle that she was not the town fool.

"Erm," she muttered.

Furiously, she searched her thoughts for the right words to mark the occasion of forming an acquaintance she had no desire to make.

A thousand quotations and aphorisms leapt to mind, but she must not speak them.

Miss Hardcastle waited, her eyes expectant.

Finally, Mary surrendered and said, "It is said that 'safety lies in virtuous friendship and rational conversation,' but I fear that is merely a paraphrase of the original."

Beside her, Mrs. Bennet groaned in disapproval, but Miss Hardcastle laughed with delight, took Mary by the arm, and led her to a sofa. "Oh, my dear new friend, what an odd thing to say! May I call you Mary?"

Before Mary could decline, Miss Hardcastle continued, "And you shall call me Penelope, for I can tell we are to be fast friends, are we not?"

Mary swallowed. Her head spun as she tried to clutch one of Miss Hardcastle's thoughts.

"Yes," Miss Hardcastle said, answering her own question. "We shall be good friends indeed. But Meryton is full of kind people, is it not? I do not believe I have visited a friendlier place in the whole of my life. Everyone I have met has been so very kind to me."

It was Mary's moment to speak, but fearing her mother's disapproval if she utilized another quotation, she blurted, "That is because you are so very beautiful. Of course, they would be kind to you."

When Mary realized what she said, her head snapped back, and she barely restrained herself from clapping both hands over her lips like a dolt.

"That is to say…," Mary sputtered, her face reddening in frustration and humiliation. Her eyes darted to her mother, and she wished a thousand times that the word "moralizing" had never been uttered. Mary seemed to possess only two options: either she must quote from her memory or let slip her most inappropriate thoughts. The former was unacceptable to her mother, and the latter was abhorrent to herself.

Finally, Mary made the only possible decision. She said, "'Ointment and perfume rejoice the heart: so doth the sweetness of a man's friend by hearty counsel.'"

"Dear Mary," Penelope said, laughing again. "You are indeed one of the oddest creatures I ever met. Your quotations put me in mind of my own dear brother, for he takes great pleasure in debating literature of all sorts. Have you been to Mr. Philips's law office to make the acquaintance of Simon?"

"I should think not!" Mary said, feeling on more comfortable footing now that she had a rule of etiquette to guide her conversation. "A young lady requires a proper introduction to make the acquaintance of any of the opposite sex, whether or not they are employed by a relation."

"Yes, of course," Penelope agreed. "It is only that I have met so many people already that it seems they must also have met my brother. Well, it is of little import. You shall be introduced, and you shall get along famously. I am certain of it."

"I look forward to making his acquaintance," Mary said by rote. She most certainly did not look forward to meeting anyone now that her communication abilities had been crippled. She would make an utter fool of herself.

Of course, if Mr. Hardcastle were anything like his sister in appearance, he would be far too handsome to look upon Mary with a friendly eye.

৵ Three ৵

"You shall be pleased to discover that Mr. Hardcastle should arrive soon," Mrs. Philips said from the opposite sofa.

With those words only just uttered, the door opened, and two gentlemen entered.

"Oh! Here is my brother now," Miss Hardcastle said, clapping her hands in delight.

Mary froze. She sat transfixed as Miss Hardcastle jumped from her seat and rushed to her brother's side, her skirt swirling around her dainty ankles.

From the other sofa, Mrs. Bennet cleared her throat, a sound that somehow managed to be fraught with meaning.

Mary's head swiveled to her mother, and she realized that she ought to have stood by now.

She rose, and the new posture seemed to impart unto her the courage to have a good look at the gentleman whom her mother, her aunt and uncle, and perhaps even his sister expected to be Mary's match.

Mr. Hardcastle stood a great deal taller than both his sister and Mr. Philips, and his pale skin sharply contrasted his close-cropped, mousy brown hair. High, sharp cheekbones slashed across his face, lending him rather hawkish features. His eyes were intelligent and alert, leaving Mary no doubt that he comprehended the true purpose of this meeting as well as she did.

But rather than appearing as awkward as Mary felt, Mr. Hardcastle projected aloof amusement as if he were merely observing a comedic scene and not taking part in it.

Mary watched silently as Mr. Philips presented Mr. Hardcastle to her mother, who smiled at the young man with obvious delight and unconcealed intent. She intended a match, and subtlety was not in her nature.

"Mr. Hardcastle, you do us great honor," Mrs. Bennet enthused. "We are ever so pleased that Mr. Philips saw fit to bring you to us, are we not, Mary?"

Mr. Hardcastle's focus shifted to Mary, and under his direct assessment, her cheeks went scarlet.

"Simon," Miss Hardcastle entreated, relieving Mary of her brother's focused intensity, if only momentarily. "Do allow me to introduce you to my dear friend."

Miss Hardcastle slid her hand into the crook of her brother's elbow and led him across the room toward Mary.

As they navigated the cluttered space, Mr. Hardcastle turned to his sister with an air of incredulity. "It perplexes me how you may make an acquaintance one moment and declare her your dear friend the next."

"For my part," Miss Hardcastle replied pertly, "I do not comprehend why *you* insist on making a stranger of everyone you encounter. Now, allow me to present Miss Bennet, for I predict that you will one day call her a friend."

Mary curtsied as Mr. Hardcastle bowed, and when she ventured a look into his eyes, she discovered that they were cast of the same sapphire blue as his sister's. However, while Miss Hardcastle looked upon the world with overt pleasure, her brother viewed the same scene with an ironical bent.

Mary gripped her skirts and wished once more that she had been aware of this scheme much earlier. Perhaps she could have avoided this unpleasant business altogether. Mr. Hardcastle clearly comprehended her mother's matrimonial intentions and likely had decided against her.

"I am pleased to make your acquaintance, Miss Bennet," Mr. Hardcastle said. Gone was the chiding tone he had used with his sister, and in its place was careful neutrality.

"And I am pleased to make your acquaintance, sir." She repeated his words, but this time, she was victorious over her fear. This time, she continued to speak, choosing a pretty subject. "How do you find Meryton?"

"Adequate," he replied, looking briefly away and offering no further explanation.

Mary pursed her lips. Now that the pretty subject of Meryton had been exhausted with Mr. Hardcastle's one-word reply, she again found herself at a loss. She had often observed her sisters in conversation with gentlemen, and though she felt sure she had little talent for flirtation, she could at least seek to be clever.

But what does one say to a gentleman whom everyone in the room intends to be her match? Should she endeavor to discuss another pretty subject? The roads? The weather?

Why did this have to be so difficult?

"Adequate?" Mr. Philips repeated with a laugh, saving Mary from her dilemma. "You have quite a talent for understatement. I am certain there are those among our acquaintance who can tempt you to a better opinion."

He winked at Mary.

Whatever relief Mary felt at Mr. Philips's interruption quickly fled, leaving pure embarrassment in its wake.

"Oh, yes!" Mrs. Bennet agreed. "We can turn his opinion, can we not, Mary?"

Mr. Hardcastle considered Mary for a moment and offered her a knowing smile. The expression held both humor and a sort of kinship, as if they were united by this embarrassment.

For both their sakes, she must do something to divert her relations, for she could not bear one more ill-concealed reference to matrimonial hopes. Caring only to ease the tension in the room, Mary said the first thing that came to mind: "'If a man does not make new acquaintances as he advances through life, he will soon find himself alone. A man should keep his friendships in constant repair.'"

Mrs. Bennet expelled a loud sigh, but Mary could not regret her error, for at least the horrid innuendo ceased.

"Ah," Mr. Hardcastle said, tipping his head to the side. "You lay upon us a quotation from the brilliant Dr. Johnson."

Mary's lips parted in shock, and she nodded.

"I have always preferred to exercise another of his dicta: 'If you are idle, be not solitary; if you are solitary, be not idle.'"

Mary's heart clenched and then accelerated, thumping with uncharacteristic ardor in her chest. Rarely had any person, be it man or lady, returned her quotation for quotation.

Her head suddenly felt light, as if she had inhaled the vapors of her mother's laudanum. She very nearly giggled.

Shocked by her own reaction, Mary stared at Mr. Hardcastle. He returned her gaze, a small smile playing about his lips.

"Speaking of idleness," Mr. Philips interrupted, "I fear Mr. Hardcastle and I may not stay for tea as promised. We have a matter of some urgency to attend. We must be off even now. I do apologize."

Mr. Hardcastle's smile turned regretful, and Mary forced herself to look away.

"Oh, Mr. Philips!" Mrs. Bennet protested. "Your laws and such can wait, surely!"

Mr. Hardcastle turned to Mrs. Bennet and gave her a gracious smile. "'We are time's subjects, and time bids be gone.'"

"Whatever do you mean by that?" Mrs. Bennet demanded, looking to Mrs. Philips for clarity.

Her aunt only shrugged.

"Shakespeare," Mary said softly to her mother. "He is quoting *Henry the Fourth*."

Mr. Hardcastle smiled fully at Mary. His mischievous eyes conveyed his amusement at Mrs. Bennet's reaction.

"What is it that Shakespeare says about lawyers?" Mrs. Philips asked, embracing the quotation game. "I can never seem to recall a passage when it is called for. I have not Mary's talent for it."

Mary's eyes flew to Mr. Hardcastle's as an utterly inappropriate quotation leapt to her lips, but she dared not speak it. She flushed and looked away.

To her great surprise, Mr. Hardcastle spoke it for her. "'The first thing we do, let's kill all the lawyers.'"

While the other ladies in the room went about making half-hearted protests, Mary returned Mr. Hardcastle's smile with a genuine smile of her own. She desired nothing more than to continue her conversation with him. She wanted to know everything about him. She wanted to make those blue eyes look upon her—only her.

Her heart raced, and her breathing was shallow.

Mary paled as she realized that she—Mary Bennet—was experiencing symptoms of romantic desire. Lust.

With terribly clarity, Mary comprehended the reasons that women were warned to guard against these violent romantic fancies.

No good could come of such wanton feelings.

༽ Four ଅ

Mrs. Bennet remained mercifully silent on the return to Longbourn, offering Mary an opportunity to reflect on all that had happened over the course of the morning. Mary stared out the coach window, but her thoughts occupied her so wholly that she did not notice when the town gave way to the beauty of the countryside.

As she had predicted, the morning indeed proved to be a disaster. And she had made her prognostication when she believed the worst development of the day was her newfound knowledge that her conversation was perceived as moralizing.

It was much worse. Her meeting with the Hardcastle siblings yielded far more dire consequences than mere awkward conversation.

Her reaction to Mr. Hardcastle resulted in a harrowing realization: Mary Bennet was capable of sentimentality.

How very humiliating a fact to discover!

The gentleman uttered one or two fine quotations, and what had Mary done? She had blushed and gawked at him just as Kitty or Lydia did when they encountered a gaggle of handsome officers.

Why, Mary might as well have giggled and swooned too.

She crossed her arms and hunched forward, still inattentive to the passing scenery. Instead, her mind's eye conjured Mr. Hardcastle's face as she attempted to discover the reasons for her reaction to him. Certainly, his features were not classically handsome, so she could not credit his appearance. They had only just been introduced and, therefore, held little conversation, so she could not claim that she truly knew his mind or character. Why then could she not be indifferent to him?

Mary stomped her foot on the coach floor, eliciting a questioning glance from Mrs. Bennet. Mary ignored her.

Her situation was unacceptable.

Mary Bennet refused to be ruled by her feelings. Such sentiments denoted a weakness of mind and a temptation toward lust and sin. Was it not said that "violent love cannot subsist, at least cannot be expressed, for any time together, on both sides, otherwise the certain consequence however concealed, is satiety and disgust"?

Lydia, her flesh-and-blood relation, had fallen victim to such unrestrained emotion.

Love claimed Elizabeth and Jane amongst its victims as well. They had not suffered to the same degree as Lydia; however, they had the good sense to fall in love with wealthy gentlemen.

Though Mary had not believed it until that very day, heredity made it probable that she would follow her sisters' course.

Alas, Mr. Hardcastle was not wealthy. He was a solicitor, a tradesman. As such, he was hardly a more suitable mate than Mr. Wickham.

Mary's eyelids slid shut, and she shook her head.

Turmoil awaited her if she gave way to her feelings. That much was certain. She intended to be guided by pure reason.

But, she reasoned, was not this match made and thus sanctioned by her mother?

Was not marrying according to her parents' wishes her duty to God?

Why, Mary ought to be thankful that she liked the chosen gentleman.

Perhaps this was the best of all possible outcomes.

Tenderness for her husband might be a fine thing, a thing for which she had never dared hope.

Why should Mary not indulge herself in a bit of fancy and romance, especially if it was sanctioned by her own family?

She would be following God's commandment to honor her father and mother. In the process of pleasing her family and honoring the Lord, she would secure her future; she could safely indulge in a bit—just a bit—of harmless sentimentality.

A grin spread across her lips as the coach ground to a halt in front of Longbourn.

Yes, everyone would be pleased, she decided as she leapt out of the carriage.

∽◎ ◎∾

Mrs. Bennet's silence could be contained no longer than it took for her to cross the threshold of Longbourn.

"Why do you not mind me, Mary?" she demanded as she tossed her pelisse from her shoulders. The garment would have fallen to the floor had Hill, their housekeeper, not been there to prevent it.

"I did just as you asked, Mama," Mary protested, surprised out of her pleasant reverie. "I did not moralize, and I spoke of pretty subjects."

"But the quotations! What could you have been thinking? No one wants to have entire novels quoted to them upon first acquaintance."

"I do not read novels!" Mary insisted as she removed her outerwear and handed it neatly to Hill. "And I did not quote copious amounts of material. Besides, Mr. Hardcastle offered quotations of his own."

Mrs. Bennet groaned and then blustered toward the sitting room.

"Tea please, Hill! I am terribly parched after such a long, dusty drive. Mary! Come and sit with me."

From her place in the hallway, Mary gazed at the stairs with longing, but she reminded herself that being noticed had always been her fondest wish and that she ought to appreciate her mother's attentions, frustrating as they could be.

After all, Mrs. Bennet had never before looked upon her middle daughter with an eye toward making a match, and Mary knew she should feel honored. She followed her mother to the cozy room, but she felt too agitated to sit. Instead, she paced beside the window.

"I must admit, however," Mrs. Bennet said as if their conversation had not been interrupted, "that Mr. Hardcastle seemed to have just as many useless quotations stored away in his head as you do. Perhaps you have done well in spite of everything."

Mrs. Bennet gave Mary a vibrant smile, but Mary's emotions were too unsettled for her to bask in her mother's praise.

"I confess—" Mary stopped her pacing and looked away from her mother as she began her admission. "I confess that I like Mr. Hardcastle."

Spoken aloud, Mary's sentiments sounded even odder than they had in the privacy of her thoughts. Feeling every bit a fool for revealing the truth of her feelings, she awaited her mother's reaction.

"Of course, you like him," Mrs. Bennet cooed. "Just as I knew you would. A mother is always right."

Mrs. Bennet did not comprehend the enormity of what Mary had just revealed.

"Now," Mrs. Bennet murmured as if Mary had quit the chamber entirely, "I must construct a method of bringing the two together. If only Mr. Hardcastle had been able to stay to tea, he might have proposed already!"

"Mama," Mary said softly, drawing her mother's notice once again. "Why did you not tell me the purpose of this morning's call? Perhaps if I had been aware that you intended Mr. Hardcastle as a match, I might have better prepared myself."

Mrs. Bennet drew her hand over her heart, and her face grew serious. "You know me, Mary. I am not the presumptuous sort. I had no notion of actually making a match. Your aunt and I had little idea that you might do so well with him."

Mary turned to face the window as she sorted out her mother's confusing messages. Somehow Mrs. Bennet had both known the match would work and believed that Mary would do something to ruin it.

With her back safely to her mother, she rolled her eyes in a most juvenile manner. That was her sole act of revolt, but it felt delightful.

Behind her, the door opened, startling the sarcastic expression from Mary's face. She turned to find that Hill had entered the room carrying a tea service. She set it on the table before Mrs. Bennet.

"A letter from Mrs. Darcy arrived in your absence," Hill said, offering the missive to Mrs. Bennet on a small silver plate. "Mr. Bennet has asked me to deliver it to your hand."

"Oh! How wonderful," Mrs. Bennet cried, eagerly reaching for the letter. "My dear, rich Lizzie! Although I do not like to boast about her wealth...."

Mrs. Bennet forgot Mary, Mr. Hardcastle, and her parching thirst in favor of the correspondence, which she unfolded immediately. Hill poured two cups of tea, crossed the room to give one to Mary, and then departed.

Mary sipped her beverage, drawing solace from its warmth and rich flavor, and listened as her mother began to read.

Rather than sharing the entire contents of the letter, Mrs. Bennet treated Mary to random words and phrases.

From what Mary could discern, Lizzie and her husband were well. Kitty had settled charmingly at Pemberley and enjoyed society in that county.

"Oh!" Mrs. Bennet gasped. "And here is some news you will want to hear, Mary!"

With her mind still preoccupied with the events of the morning, Mary tried to muster some curiosity about her sister's news. Perhaps Lizzie was soon to be a mother. It was the natural progression.

"Mr. Darcy has offered to settle a large dowry upon Kitty!" Mrs. Bennet paused and shrieked. "Ten thousand pounds! Ten thousand!"

Mary's ears ached at the sound of her mother's delight.

"Imagine it, Mary!" Mrs. Bennet began to fan herself and giggle convulsively. "Now, not only shall Kitty be in the path of rich men, but she shall have an inducement to draw them in."

Mary could hardly figure how that news was to interest her. An unexpected benefit for one of her sisters was neither new nor surprising. They always received offers of holidays and travel and money while Mary sat at home.

"But that is not the best bit!" Mrs. Bennet proclaimed. "You too, Mary, will benefit from Lizzie's fortuitous marriage. Mr. Darcy shall provide you with a dowry of equal measure to Kitty's!"

The blood drained from Mary's extremities in an alarming rush, and she nearly dropped the teacup she held.

"A large dowry?" Mary repeated. "Ten thousand pounds?"

That sum exceeded her own father's annual income by a factor of five!

"Why!" Mrs. Bennet exclaimed. "With this additional lure, you shall not have to settle for a lowly law clerk!"

Mary blinked hard and deposited her teacup and saucer on the first available surface. She had hardly gotten acquainted with the idea of Mr. Hardcastle as a suitor, and now her mother was removing him from consideration.

And she did like Mr. Hardcastle.

"But—"

"Only think of it, Mary! Now you may attain a landed gentleman. Or perhaps you may gain a gentleman of title." She waved a hand as if to erase her words. "No, not a title. That is too much for a girl with your looks. Yet you will have so many prospects. We must announce that you have money, and the gentlemen shall arrive in droves."

Suddenly too weak to support her own weight, Mary dropped to the nearest chair. She cared nothing for property, houses, or titles. She had liked Mr. Hardcastle, the lowly law clerk.

"Well, what have you to say, dear girl?" her mother asked, eyes bright as she surveyed her middle daughter over the letter she still held.

"I— I—" Mary stuttered.

"Never fear, my dear! I will take care of every detail. I shall write to your aunt immediately. This cannot keep until the morrow. We must spread the word even now!"

"But Mr. Hardcastle?" Mary managed to ask, her voice barely above a whisper.

Mrs. Bennet folded the letter, placed it on the table, and picked up her tea.

"Mr. Hardcastle indeed!" she sniffed with newfound disdain in her voice. "Who is Mr. Hardcastle? I have already quite forgotten him."

Mary slumped farther down in the chair. Mrs. Bennet's elated remarks droned in the background, but Mary could not help thinking that perhaps she did not want to forget Mr. Hardcastle as quickly as her mother had.

≈৹ Five ৹≈

Not half an hour later, Mary hovered in the doorway of her father's study. Overwhelmed by the changes she had experienced in one short morning, she found that her world had shifted yet again with the announcement of Mr. Darcy's dowry. Mary simply could not grasp it all.

Upon noticing his daughter's uncharacteristic behavior, Mr. Bennet laid his book aside.

"Child, do come here," he beckoned from behind his large, cluttered desk. "You have heard, I can see, of Mr. Darcy's generous offer."

Mary padded into her father's sacred chamber and stood before him clutching at her skirt.

"Yes, Papa," she said. "I confess it has left me feeling rather bewildered."

"Your mother is no doubt already sounding the alert."

Mary nodded. "She has written to Aunt Philips, and the letter is *en route* even now." She paused, considering her words carefully. "I cannot help but think that her announcement of my newfound wealth is…impetuous."

"Indeed." Mr. Bennet laughed lightly. "Your mother is nothing if not impetuous. I fear little could be done to prevent her from spreading such news as this. We may as well allow her to bask in the glory of Mr. Darcy's generosity."

Mary grimaced. Her father, though calm and even-tempered, valued his peace too highly.

Still, he was probably correct. Nothing—not even an injunction from God himself—could have prevented Mrs. Bennet from displaying her good fortune, but that did not justify such a public announcement.

"But, Papa, are we not exhorted to avoid boasting? I have read a great deal on this subject."

Mr. Bennet offered Mary a small smile and then gestured to the chair across from his desk. "Sit yourself down, my dear."

Mary's lips parted in surprise, and she took the proffered seat with reverence she usually reserved for a church pew. Many a time had she passed this very door to find Elizabeth so situated and in quiet conversation with their father, but rare were the times when Mary had occupied this place. She ran a hand along the wooden arm of the chair, determined to make the most of the opportunity.

"Your mother has many faults," Mr. Bennet said. "But she believes herself to be doing right by you."

"I know, Papa."

Mrs. Bennet always had the best of intentions, but they did not always produce the corresponding results. Lydia was testament to that fact.

"Mr. Darcy's dowry has given you a certain freedom," Mr. Bennet continued. "Limited options were previously available to you."

Mary understood what her father had been kind enough to leave unsaid. She was plain and awkward, and until now, she had no dowry. Therefore, she possessed none of the qualities that attracted gentlemen. A dowry made Mary Bennet desirable.

Her heart clenched at that thought. She did not want to be taken as a liability. She wanted her future husband to like her more than her money.

"It is said that money is the root of all evil," Mary stated, finally voicing her fear in the only way she could. "Will it not attract gentlemen with mercenary motives?"

Mr. Bennet's eyes narrowed briefly as he considered his middle daughter. "You fear that anyone who courts you would only be pursuing Mr. Darcy's money and thus be evil?"

Mary nodded, looking away from her father's assessing gaze.

"I believe you have been done a disservice, child," he said, his gray-tinged eyebrows drawn down in contemplation. "You have been allowed to disappear into your studies too long without guidance. You have acquired a great deal of information, but you lack the guidance to help you develop that knowledge into true wisdom."

Mary met his frown. "I do not take your meaning. I have studied and gained all the proper accomplishments. I am aware of the ways of the world. I simply do not know if I approve of them."

"We have failed to teach you what it is to live in a time and place such as ours. Now that you are the only of our offspring at home, you shall have the benefit of all that you lacked as a child. Listen well, for here is the first lesson I have to teach you."

Mary nodded, eager to hear the wisdom of her father.

"You have misunderstood the verse you summarized earlier. The *love* of money is the root of all evil, not money itself. Mr. Darcy's money has the potential to make you secure for the rest of your days, dear girl. Consider what may become of you after your mother and I expire. The house is entailed upon your cousin Mr. Collins, and your mother will be forced upon one of your sisters. If you remain unmarried, you shall become their dependent as well."

"Spinsters who seek refuge in the homes of relatives become little more than servants."

Mary had not the least wish to be seen and yet unnoticed in one of her sister's households.

"For good or ill," Mr. Bennet said, "money buys marriage, which brings security, and you must not discount or fear that. We must accept reality for what it is. A wealthy man rarely marries a poor woman, for he must shore up his wealth. And a landed gentleman must not be allowed to consider a poor woman, for he has many laborers to support. He may lose his family's living altogether. Not all who seek your fortune are evil. A gentleman will use your fortune for good, and he will not neglect his duty to care for you. Some—those who are poor, who gamble, or who labor in trade—may seek you for nefarious reasons. You must be wary."

Mr. Hardcastle's visage leapt into Mary's mind, and she dismissed it quickly. Her father was correct. No sensible woman bound herself to a tradesman if she could possibly help it, no matter what sentiments he elicited in her heart.

A sensible woman did not allow emotion to guide her, and Mary was nothing if not a sensible woman.

"Thanks to your mother's helpful dissemination of information, suitors will come. Some will be mercenary and full of avarice, and some will have more prudent motives." Here, Mr. Bennet paused and gave Mary a meaningful look. "You and Kitty have an advantage over your sisters, for Mr. Darcy's dowry frees you. You shall have your pick of the gentlemen now, child. But choose wisely which of them is worthy of you."

Mr. Bennet leaned back in his chair and regarded Mary with an artless expression.

"Do you comprehend me, Mary?" he asked. "Choose for yourself whom you will wed."

"I—I believe I understand, Papa," she said. He had said plainly that she ought to question the motives of her suitors, but something beyond the literal hid in his words, something that eluded her.

Again, Mr. Hardcastle leapt to mind, and Mary blushed. Feeling foolish for allowing herself to think upon him, Mary rose, exited her father's study, and took refuge in her bedchamber, closing the door behind her with a soft click. Her father told her to accept reality as it was, and she must do that.

She must face the truth.

Mr. Hardcastle was not the gentleman for her.

ꙮ Six ꙮ

Once the news of Mary's dowry spread, suitors appeared. Although Mrs. Bennet's prediction about the size of the horde of gentleman was greatly overestimated, they were indeed drawn by the lure of money.

At first, Mary felt the absurdity of the situation with particular keenness.

She could not ignore the fact that she had been flung upon the marriage market as a liability, something to be taken only because the financial incentive proved attractive enough.

But as the days passed, Mary seemed to rise in the esteem of Meryton society in general. She could not prevent herself from feeling flattered. Moreover, her mother's joy could not be contained within the walls of Longbourn.

Each morning, Mary sat with her mother in Mrs. Philips's sitting room and listened as Mrs. Bennet discussed her marital prospects. This morning, Miss Hardcastle had joined them.

Though Mary had begun to enjoy these mornings, she could not decide how to behave in Miss Hardcastle's presence. Before the change in her financial circumstances, Mr. Hardcastle had been the focus of Mrs. Bennet's matchmaking, and now he was no longer an option.

Miss Hardcastle must be aware of this fact, though Mary's aunt and mother seemed to have forgotten it. They continued to discuss gentlemen without regard for the young woman whose brother had been removed from consideration.

For her part, Miss Hardcastle appeared unconcerned. She read quietly as the other women talked around her.

"My dear," Mrs. Bennet crooned to her daughter, "I knew one day you would shine like your sisters! Finally, *this* is your time. Many a mother has offered up her son as a potential match, but I am careful. I shall only allow the best to pursue you."

"I should not feel half so flattered as I do," Mary mused aloud. "Mere days ago these gentlemen were strangers to me, and I have met none of them in person."

"Pooh!" Mrs. Bennet said. "Why must you be so serious, Mary? Can you not enjoy being admired for the first time in your life?"

"Indeed, child," Mrs. Philips said. "Your mother will not pack you off to the first suitor who steps through the door. We shall find the proper gentleman."

Mary glanced guiltily at Miss Hardcastle, who looked up from her book long enough to offer her a small smile.

"How am I to know the proper gentleman unless I first make his acquaintance?" Mary asked her mother.

"Oh!" Mrs. Bennet huffed, exhaling so forcefully that the curls around her face fluttered in the breeze. "You see, Sister! You see what I must endure. Mary is ever taxing my nerves and ruining anything that is amusing."

"No, Mary is quite correct," Mrs. Philips said with a terrifying gleam in her eyes. "Mary ought to meet her suitors."

Sensing her sister's devilish intent, Mrs. Bennet leaned forward, causing deep creases in her gown that Hill would be required to remove later.

"Let us have a small dinner party in Mary's honor," Mrs. Philips proposed.

Mary inhaled sharply as emotions—elation, fear, longing, regret—swelled all at once within her.

To be the guest of honor at a dinner party—to be the center of attention, to be seen—that was more than she had ever dreamed.

"A party!" Mrs. Bennet exclaimed, giggling. "I am ever in favor of a party. Mary, what say you?"

Before Mary could respond, her aunt spoke again.

"And of course, it would also serve to introduce Mr. and Miss Hardcastle to the neighborhood at large. Perhaps we might make three matches!"

Three matches? They now intended to match Mr. Hardcastle with someone else?

What a terrible idea!

"What an excellent idea!" Mrs. Bennet proclaimed. "We shall invite only those who are deemed acceptable suitors." She turned to Miss Hardcastle as though she were one of her royal subjects. "But do not fear, Miss Hardcastle. After Mary has made her selection of gentleman, there shall be more than enough left over for you."

Mary blanched at her mother's thoughtless words, but Miss Hardcastle smiled at Mrs. Bennet.

"How very kind of you to think of me and my brother," she said with only a hint of stiffness.

Oblivious to her offense, Mrs. Bennet nodded graciously and returned her attention to her newfound task. "Now, whom shall we invite?"

"We ought to write a list of each gentleman and his assets," Mrs. Philips added helpfully. "If I recall correctly, Mr. Sewell has two thousand a year...."

Now that her mother and aunt had conceived of this idea, they would not rest until they listed the financial value and acreage of every eligible gentleman in the county.

"Mary," Miss Hardcastle beckoned from her spot across the room, "I know you are engaged in conversation, but would it trouble you overmuch to help me navigate this difficult passage? I can make nothing sensible of it."

Miss Hardcastle held up the book, but Mary could not discern the title from such a distance.

"What do you read, Miss Hardcastle?" Mary asked as she stood and walked across the room, dodging a stool *en route*. She dearly hoped it to be a tome with which she was acquainted, perhaps Fordyce.

"Penelope," Miss Hardcastle corrected her.

Despite the fact that she had no intention of using the familiar appellation, Mary nodded and reached for the book. Miss Hardcastle refused to relinquish it for Mary's perusal. Instead, she kept it within her grasp, leaned near, and whispered, "I brought you across the room under false pretenses."

Mary blinked. "You have no need for interpretive opinion?"

"Oh no!" Miss Hardcastle said, flipping the book shut. "This is merely some tripe I pulled from Mrs. Philips's shelf."

Mary recognized it as one of her aunt's Gothic romance novels. She had never read a book of that particular genre, but her sisters often indulged in them. It seemed just the sort of book that would suit Miss Hardcastle.

"I can think of no one who would have trouble understanding the plot of this novel," Miss Hardcastle continued. "It is ever so predictable: crumbling castles, a mysterious figure in the night, and a romance continually thwarted by circumstance. The only question I have is whether or not I shall bother continuing to the conclusion, for it seems that I can now predict it. But is not that part of the charm of such a book? Though I can guess the ending, I yet worry about the heroine's happiness."

"I suppose so," Mary said. It sounded like errant nonsense to her, and she thought to say so. Glancing at her mother and aunt, Mary found them engaged in list-making and decided it better not to risk offending Miss Hardcastle by insulting her choice of reading material. "Why have you lured me here?"

"May I speak plainly?" she asked, patting the seat beside her.

"Please," Mary said, sitting obediently. "I greatly prefer plain speech to innuendo. It leaves less room for discomfort."

"I hoped we might escape for a few moments," Miss Hardcastle confessed in a quiet voice. "Shall we not walk about Meryton?"

Mary's brows drew down in confusion and then realization struck. Miss Hardcastle must be uncomfortable with her mother and aunt's choice of conversational topics. Mary concealed a smirk. If only her mother knew that her conversation was found wanting, and Miss Hardcastle sought Mary's company instead.

༒ Seven ༒

The two young women hardly stepped from Mrs. Philips's front door before Miss Hardcastle linked their arms together and said, "Forgive me if my forthcoming remark intrudes on your privacy, but I agree with you, Mary. You ought to meet your suitors before a marriage settlement is made. We are not living in the Middle Ages when women were chattel. It is no longer in fashion for parents to decide a child's matrimonial future."

Unused to such intimate contact and conversation, Mary felt ill at ease and barely restrained herself from removing her hand from Miss Hardcastle's grasp. She walked steadily and silently, maintaining a strict focus on the bustling town around them.

Midmorning had come and gone, and the tradesmen had long been about their labor. Shopkeepers bustled about, hawking their wares. Mary glanced with abhorrence at the millinery shop, a favorite of all her sisters, and in anticipation of being dragged within its confines, she prepared a demurral. But Miss Hardcastle hardly spared a look at the bonnets and ribbons displayed in the window.

She still awaited a reply, so Mary spoke her mind truthfully. "I do not believe my family intends to sell me off.

They simply wish me to marry for practical reasons, for security. But I do confess to mixed thoughts on the subject."

Miss Hardcastle gave her a practical look. "Do you not wish to fall in love and be married?"

"I hardly know," Mary confessed. Unaccustomed to having emotions and even less accustomed to speaking about them, she said the first thing that came to her mind: "Marriage is an estate settled upon us by God, so I must not disapprove of it."

A small laugh burst from Miss Hardcastle's lips.

"Why do you laugh?" Mary asked, pulling at her arm and finding Miss Hardcastle's grip unbreakable. "I have said nothing so very humorous."

Miss Hardcastle shook her head, still smiling. "You have told me God's opinion, but what are *your* thoughts on the subject?"

Mary did not comprehend her meaning. "I have just told you my opinion."

Miss Hardcastle appeared as if she might argue the point, but finally, she asked, "Have you never been in love?"

"In love?" Mary repeated, her voice dropping low so that passersby might not hear. Her mind drifted back to those weeks when her cousin Mr. Collins had visited Longbourn.

Mary would have accepted his proposal with gladness, for the sacrifice would have saved her family. As her father's heir, Mr. Collins would inherit Longbourn upon Mr. Bennet's death, thus leaving the females of the family without shelter or protection. Had Mary secured Mr. Collins, she would have likewise secured their futures. She would have won her parents' eternal gratitude, and she would have had the prestige of being the first of the five Bennet sisters to be wed.

Mary would finally have been valued.

All that would have occurred had Mr. Collins sought her hand in marriage.

But he had not.

Instead, Mr. Collins had considered every other woman within the district, always excepting Mary, who was under his beaky nose all the time. Instead, he had wed Charlotte Lucas, their neighbor.

Beside Mary, Miss Hardcastle said, "I must interpret your pause to mean that some gentleman from your past has wronged you."

"There was a gentleman," Mary admitted slowly.

Miss Hardcastle laughed again, a joyful sound that caused Mary to frown. "Just as I said! There is romance in your past."

Mary did not often speak with such intimacy to anyone, and she felt herself blush. "There was no romance. Nor did he wrong me. He—he did not recognize me."

Miss Hardcastle raised a blonde brow. "I do not take your meaning."

"I did not expect you would," Mary said, her tone blunter than she intended. "Your beauty is recognized wherever you go. I seem to blend into the background. I think you may be the only person outside of my own relations who has ever held a conversation with me."

Miss Hardcastle began to walk again, her arm still firmly joined with Mary's, and they continued in silence for some minutes.

"So this gentleman," she said softly. "Were you in love with him?"

Mary conjured an image of Mr. Collins. Though she could have been prevailed upon to marry him, she had been keenly aware of his defects. She discerned a solidity in his reflections, but the truth was that he was not half so clever as herself. Mary, however, had believed that if she encouraged him to read and improve himself by such an example as hers, he might become a very agreeable companion.

"I am too practical for bouts of feeling," Mary said, her words intended to persuade Miss Hardcastle as well as herself.

Miss Hardcastle only nodded, and a few steps later, they reached the door of Mr. Philips's law office.

"And here we are," Miss Hardcastle announced.

Shock and panic hit Mary in a unified blow. Miss Hardcastle had brought them to the very last threshold she wanted to cross.

She stopped, jerking Miss Hardcastle to a halt as well, and glared at the faded wooden sign that swung gently above the door.

"I—I have no reason to call upon my uncle!" Mary protested as she attempted to take a step backward.

Miss Hardcastle tightened her grip on Mary's arm. "Who mentioned your uncle? I have come to pay a call upon my brother."

Mary's eyebrows flew toward her hairline. She must forget Mr. Hardcastle and the strange feelings he elicited in her. She simply could not see him.

"My uncle will not appreciate an interruption at this hour," Mary said, hoping to strike upon an argument that would end her companion's nonsensical plot.

"Nor will my brother!" Miss Hardcastle said with glee, pulling Mary inexorably forward. "He despises interruptions of any sort at any hour. That is precisely why we must call upon him. It will be ever so entertaining. He will do his best to appear annoyed with me, but do not fret. It does not follow that he will be annoyed with you."

"Why ever should I care if your brother became annoyed at me?" Mary squeaked, knowing she protested too much.

Miss Hardcastle smiled and dropped Mary's arm. Then, she whirled and flung open the door of the law office, eliciting the excited chiming of the bell that hung above the door.

Surprised by her sudden freedom, Mary stared at the back of Miss Hardcastle's blue and white day gown as it disappeared into the building.

Of their own accord, Mary's feet took her inside. She halted just inside the doorway, hands clutched in front of her as she awaited her uncle's reception.

Mr. Philips looked up from his worktable. He pushed his shaggy, graying hair from his eyes.

"Mary!" he said, surprise, or perhaps frustration, rendering his voice a higher pitch. He stood and rounded the large table. "What do you do here? Has your mother sent you on some errand or other? Would that she could have waited until the workday was done."

Wondering why no one ever acted as if they were pleased to see her, Mary gripped her hands tighter and prepared to issue an apology for her unexpected visit.

Beside her, Miss Hardcastle cleared her throat, a dainty sound that drew both her attention and Mr. Philips's.

Her uncle's eyes swung toward Miss Hardcastle and lingered there for some seconds. Miss Hardcastle curtsied as though to the Prince Regent himself, and she finished her gesture by peering up at their host through her long, wispy eyelashes.

"Oh," Mr. Philips said, his face lighting in a smile. "I did not see you there, Miss Hardcastle."

Miss Hardcastle returned his smile with deliberate slowness.

"Good morning, Mr. Philips," she purred. "I do hope you shall not turn us away, for we have walked quite a little distance."

"Certainly not," he returned, clearing his throat so loudly that the sound echoed through the quiet of the office. "How could I not receive two such lovely young women?"

"You are too kind," Miss Hardcastle said, casting a look about the empty chamber. "We have come to see my brother.

Only for a moment, of course, for we know you have business to attend."

"He is about his labors in the back room. Please, do sit down," Mr. Philips said, gesturing to a small wooden bench positioned beside the door. "I shall send your brother to you forthwith."

Mary plunked down on the hard bench beside Miss Hardcastle while Mr. Philips disappeared into the back room of the small establishment. She stared at her dull gray skirt and listened to the murmur of masculine voices, though she could not make out their words.

"You see!" Miss Hardcastle whispered cheerily. "I assured you of our welcome. A dash of flirtation renders most gentlemen highly amenable to any request."

Mary's head snapped up sharply, and she scrutinized her friend.

"My brother will be ever so pleased that *you* have come." Miss Hardcastle winked at her. "And here he is now."

Indeed, Mr. Hardcastle's footsteps approached.

Even before she turned her eyes upon him, Mary's heart leapt, and she became overly conscious of her posture, her clothing, her every action. Each breath she drew sounded quick, labored. She felt every bit the fool that she was.

She did not even know Mr. Hardcastle, had exchanged barely three sentences with him. She should not feel such attraction. Surely, this was temptation, and she should flee it.

Mr. Hardcastle strode into the room and stopped before the bench, his ink-stained fingers clenched into fists at his sides.

"Penelope! What in God's name do you do here?" he demanded as his sister rose. Mary followed suit, her action drawing Mr. Hardcastle's notice.

"Oh," Mr. Hardcastle said, his hands relaxing at his sides. "Pardon me."

"As you see, Brother," Miss Hardcastle said, giving Mary a gentle nudge with her elbow, "I have brought my dear friend Mary with me."

Mr. Hardcastle's sharp features softened, and his cheeks were faintly flushed. Or perhaps Mary simply imagined them tinged with color.

"I perceive Miss Bennet's presence," Mr. Hardcastle said to his sister, though his attention remained on Mary. "Good morning, Miss Bennet."

He bowed, and Mary curtsied.

When he spoke again, his voice held a note of irony. "I see my sister has seen fit to bring you as her shield."

"Good morning, Mr. Hardcastle," Mary said, after which she could not think of what to say, for she could not hear her own thoughts over the hammering of her stupid heart.

"You ought to chastise my sister," he continued, "for she is utilizing you in a most shocking way."

"What do you mean, sir?" Mary asked.

"Do not be so dramatic, Simon," Miss Hardcastle protested. "I have done no such thing. You will have her distrusting me."

"So you deny that you have used her presence to mitigate my scolding of you for violating my working time?"

"I have no wish to deny it!" Miss Hardcastle said. "Besides, you are scolding me now, so my ploy has failed."

Mr. Hardcastle gave his sister a hard look, which did not cow her at all.

"For what reason have you come?" he asked.

When Miss Hardcastle did not respond immediately, he added, "Please tell me that you have come for some reason other than to amuse yourself, Sister."

Mary's suspicions were obviously correct. Miss Hardcastle hoped to make a match despite Mrs. Bennet's change of mind. Mr. Hardcastle clearly knew it too. Even though they all knew the truth, it certainly could not be spoken aloud.

Miss Hardcastle appeared stumped, however, and under Mr. Hardcastle's scrutiny, Mary blurted, "We have come to issue you an invitation. My aunt is hosting a small dinner party."

Mary had just committed half a dozen social infractions, but it was the least embarrassing option she could conjure in the moment. Once she said the words, Mary realized that she could not force herself to regret them, for she desired to know him better.

"So it is Mrs. Philips's party," Mr. Hardcastle clarified, grinning at her, "and *you* have seen fit to invite me?"

Mary flushed.

"Do not tease Miss Bennet," Miss Hardcastle said, coming valiantly to Mary's aid. "She is not accustomed to your odd sense of humor. Besides, Mrs. Philips issued the invitation herself. We merely serve as her messengers."

"Ah," he said to his sister. "'You, minion, are too saucy.' You ever have a plausible reason for your ill behavior." He then turned again to Mary. "What say you to this?"

"To *The Two Gentlemen of Verona*?" Mary asked, drawing confidence from his quotation. "Or your sister's behavior? I can find nothing suitable to say on the latter subject."

"Oh!" Miss Hardcastle said with a laugh. "Do not take his position."

"You are right, Miss Bennet," Mr. Hardcastle said, ignoring his sister. "Nothing can be said in her defense. She will never cease breaking with tradition, and that is why I adore her."

"That cannot be true," Mary said, suddenly passionate. "I have read my whole life that a woman is to show restraint and decorum. One who breaks with tradition shows neither."

"Oh, come, Mary! You cannot mean that!" Miss Hardcastle said with a mixture of surprise and confusion.

Mary shifted to face Miss Hardcastle, but it was Mr. Hardcastle who spoke next.

"Indeed, I must agree with my sister, for you, Miss Bennet, strike me as a less-than-traditional woman."

Mary whirled back to Mr. Hardcastle. It was as if he had been able to read her confusion, see her attraction to him, and confirm that she was not of strong moral character. Just as all those sermons had warned her.

Mary's horror must have been evident on her face, for he quickly added, "Moreover, it is a quality I greatly admire."

"You accuse me of being an immodest, outspoken woman?" Mary demanded. "And you claim to admire those qualities?"

Mr. Hardcastle's expression now reflected horror as well. His eyes widened in supplication.

"No, indeed," he said, taking a step forward, palms up. "I do apologize for my poor word choice. I would never accuse you of being immodest, Miss Bennet, but you are far from being the ignorant female that society demands. I fear your comments on literature reveal you to be a woman of learning."

Mary's lips dropped open as she absorbed his meaning.

Every book on the subject of women's conduct exhorted her sex to be genteel, restrained, pious, and to appear less mentally vigorous than their male counterparts. A lady must be informed and well read, but she must not reveal it.

Furthermore, gentlemen desired a young woman to display modesty and reserve, not knowledge.

According to those same texts, any man who claimed otherwise—to desire directness in a young lady—was insincere.

Mary's lips drew down in a frown and creases formed in her forehead.

"Perhaps frankness may render a lady more agreeable at first," she said, paraphrasing, "but it will surely make her less amiable as a woman."

"Piffle!" Miss Hardcastle exclaimed. "I would wager my life that those sentiments were first expressed by a man."

"Dr. John Gregory, in fact, said something very like that," Mr. Hardcastle said. "And I would readily dispute him. No gentleman wants a wife who pretends to be other than precisely who she is."

"Everything I have read disputes that claim, sir," Mary objected, her voice faltering slightly. "They declare any gentleman who professes otherwise to be a liar."

Mary did not know what response she expected from Mr. Hardcastle, but it certainly was not what she received.

He leaned closer, eyes very serious, filling her field of vision almost entirely.

"I assure you, Miss Bennet," he whispered for her ears alone, "that I am no liar. I like you just as you are."

For the barest moment, Mary's body ceased to function. The beat of her heart, the intake of her breath, the functioning of her mind: everything stopped and then rushed back ruthlessly, all at once. Her dry lips parted, but she continued to meet his eyes.

Mr. Hardcastle righted himself, stepped back, and looked toward his sister, a transition for which Mary felt inordinately grateful.

"Your usurped invitation has been given," Mr. Hardcastle said to her, his tone returning to its former lightness. "Are you quite finished interrupting my day?"

"Yes, quite," Miss Hardcastle trilled before flinging her arms around her brother, who stood frozen at the ebullient gesture.

"Then, be gone with you," he said with a hint of amusement in his voice. "Before I become unpleasant."

Miss Hardcastle and Mary did as he bade. While his sister left with a heart full of admiration, Mary left with a confused heart and an unsettled mind.

❧ ❧

Trailing after Miss Hardcastle through the streets of Meryton, Mary hurried forward and grasped her friend by the arm.

"Miss Hardcastle," Mary said, stopping her forward progress in front of the millinery shop. "Wait a moment, please."

"Certainly," Miss Hardcastle said, turning to the shop window. "Do you require a new hat?"

Mary heard the slyness in her voice.

"Of course not," Mary said. "I need to ask you an utterly impertinent question."

"I do so love impertinence," Miss Hardcastle said. "What do you need to ask?"

"Your brother?"

"Yes, Simon." Miss Hardcastle nodded expectantly.

"And you...."

She nodded again. "And me...."

"Well," Mary began, deciding to avoid any artifice. "You must be aware of my mother's earlier attempt to make a match between us."

Miss Hardcastle chuckled merrily. "Indeed, Mrs. Philips told me of the plan outright."

Mary's cheeks heated. Her aunt had been that candid?

"Even if she had not," Miss Hardcastle continued, "the plan was not well concealed enough to fool anyone who paid the least attention."

Mary's eyes slid shut in dismay.

"And your brother...he knows too?"

Miss Hardcastle shrugged. "He pays attention," she said.

"Oh, dear Lord," Mary murmured. "I am ever so embarrassed."

"Why?" Miss Hardcastle asked softly, her tone genuinely caring. "Why would you feel any sort of embarrassment at all? Is matchmaking uncommon here in Meryton?"

Mary thought back to all the matches her mother had endeavored to make over the years.

"No, it is quite common."

"I approve of the idea. You and my brother are well suited."

"Well suited?" Mary repeated.

"You are both peculiar in the same way. You read a good deal, are educated, and speak with an unusual candor that appeals to us both."

Horrified at this assessment of her character, Mary whispered, "No. This cannot be."

Miss Hardcastle's face went blank. "You do not like my brother?"

Overwhelmed and confused, Mary spoke without self-censorship. "It is not that. I like Mr. Hardcastle. I do. But I must not!"

৩৫৫ Eight ৩৫৫

Locked in her bedchamber with books piled about her, Mary spent the days prior to Mrs. Philips's dinner party in focused study and frantic contemplation.

Mr. Hardcastle's words refused to budge from her mind. He claimed to admire frankness and education in a woman.

But that could not possibly be the truth.

No one admired a woman who displayed overt intelligence or accomplishments.

That fact was indisputable, for Mary had been its victim many times. When she offered a scrap of knowledge to one of her sisters, her words were discounted with a condescending headshake or outright correction.

When she lingered too long at the pianoforte, her father removed her from the stool.

And only recently, her mother counseled her against moralizing, and what was moralizing but an overt display of knowledge?

Teeth gritted in frustration, Mary riffled through the pages of the book nearest her. Then, she slammed it shut. Every one of these tomes taught the same lessons.

A woman should be intelligent but humble. She must not outshine the gentlemen in her company. She must limit herself to pretty topics.

A woman must engage in pious reflection. She must become accustomed to confinement and readily accede to the will of others.

A woman must have talents and display them, but only within a particular limit. She must not linger overlong at the pianoforte.

Society exhorted women to bow to these lessons, but Mr. Hardcastle claimed he admired the opposite. He admired directness. And he admired these traits in Mary herself.

It was all so confounding!

His obvious affection for his own sister, who bent the will of others to her liking, seemed to prove the truth of his words. Miss Hardcastle could not be termed pious, and she certainly was not given to reflection and contemplation. Why, she had manipulated Mr. Philips with her femininity and been quite pleased with herself. Was not that sinful behavior?

Yet Mr. Hardcastle adored her.

Mary opened the nearest book to the place she had marked earlier.

"The men will complain of your reserve. They will assure you that a franker behavior would make you more amiable. But, trust me, they are not sincere when they tell you so. I acknowledge that on some occasions it might render you more agreeable as companions, but it would make you less amiable as women; an important distinction, which many of your sex are unaware of."

There was the warning, plain as ink on paper.

Gentlemen lied, and they sullied the reputations of young women.

Was Mr. Hardcastle another Mr. Wickham, a tempter?

Even the logical portion of Mary's mind told her that this could not be the case. Mr. Hardcastle had apparently approved of her before Mr. Darcy's dowry had come to be common knowledge.

But this was not Mary's worst problem. His assessment of her character tore at her soul.

If Mr. Hardcastle was accurate in his observation that Mary displayed her intelligence and accomplishments immodestly, then she had failed herself and her family in the most horrific manner possible.

Mary slammed that book closed as well and buried her face in her palms. Everything contradicted everything else, and she simply did not know what to do.

❧ ❧

Against her better judgment, Mary went to her mother's bedchamber and tapped at the door.

"Who is there?" Mrs. Bennet cried as if she feared the house might have been overtaken by barbarians.

"It is me, Mama," Mary said with a sigh.

"Mary? Do come inside, and stop that infernal tapping. It is ever so taxing on my poor nerves."

Mary rolled her eyes, regretting her decision to seek her mother's counsel, but she entered anyway.

Mrs. Bennet reclined on the bed in a lacy white gown and cap. Encircled by pillows, she all but disappeared amid the bed linens. She raised sharp blue eyes to her daughter and took in her disheveled appearance and red-rimmed eyes.

"Is something the matter, Mary?" she asked, her voice softer.

At her mother's unexpected concern, tears threatened to spill down Mary's cheeks.

"What is it, my dear?" Mrs. Bennet asked, truly concerned.

Mary edged closer to the bed and sat gently upon it. "Ever since Mr. Darcy made his offer of a dowry, I have felt unsettled. I have never before had suitors, and I fear that I might make a mistake. I do not want to disappoint you, Mama."

Or myself, she added internally.

Mrs. Bennet laid a consoling hand on Mary's arm. Surprised at the uncharacteristically maternal gesture, Mary stared mutely at her mother's fingertips.

"You think far too much," Mrs. Bennet declared. "I can see that you have turned this matter over and over in your poor mind. Too much thinking results in nothing but damage. Why, your eyes are red and your skin is sallow. If you ponder this much longer, you will be quite as homely as Charlotte Lucas."

Mary did not bother reminding her mother that homely Charlotte had lately married.

They sat in silence as Mrs. Bennet continued to stroke her arm.

"Shall I tell you what to think?" Mrs. Bennet asked at length.

For once, Mary thought it might be nice to hear her mother's advice. She nodded.

"I too have given the matter of your dowry a great deal of thought, my dear, and I believe that Mr. Randall is the prize you must seek."

"Mr. Randall?" Mary repeated in surprise.

"Yes, Mr. George Randall. He is the perfect gentleman. As he is the only son of a widower, you will have no mother-in-law to trouble you. And he is the heir to the large estate of Ashworth."

Mrs. Bennet squeezed Mary's arm with obvious excitement. She had briefly fantasized about purchasing Ashworth as a residence for Lydia after her scandalous marriage to Mr. Wickham, but that was impossible for ever so many reasons, chief among them the fact that the property was not for sale.

But perhaps a Bennet's becoming the mistress of Ashworth was no longer impossible.

Mary considered the idea and shrugged. She might very well be happy as mistress of Ashworth. By all accounts, it was a fine property with a well-stocked library. The house was situated at a reasonable distance from Meryton and Longbourn, making it possible to remain near her parents.

As to Mr. George Randall himself, however, Mary was less certain. She knew little of him except what she had heard from the local gossips.

It was said that the elder Mr. Randall—Mr. John Randall—had been quite the romantic. He had fallen in love with and consequently married a rich, young French woman. Alas, proximity often makes enemies of lovers. That seemed to be the case with Mr. John Randall and his new bride. Upon his acquiring Ashworth and setting her up as its mistress, Mr. Randall promptly fell out of love with her.

Still, they managed to conceive a son, whom Mrs. Randall insisted be called by her decidedly French surname: Beauharnais.

Much to Mr. Randall's distress, with the advent of the Napoleonic Wars came the obvious conundrum: could the son of a British gentleman be called by the same name as Napoleon's mistress? Would not his family be called out as French sympathizers? Or worse?

Fortunately for Mr. Randall, he was only required to endure the offensive name for the space of a few years. Upon his wife's death, he had absolutely forbidden anyone ever pronouncing his son's Christian name again.

Instead, he began calling the boy George after none other than the British king himself.

Having lost all faith in both love and the institution of marriage, Mr. Randall always kept young George well clear of the local young ladies.

"Have you not listened to a word your aunt and I have spoken this week?" Mrs. Bennet asked, interrupting Mary's musings on the Randall family. "Mr. Randall has been our constant subject. His estate alone, Mary! Think of it. And think of what Lady Lucas will say when she hears that my daughter is mistress of Ashworth, the finest house in the county! Oh, she may peer about Longbourn, awaiting your father's death, but I shall have the finest house in the whole county."

"You believe Mr. Randall to be a practical choice for a husband?" Mary asked.

Her mother's response was of great importance to her, for she simply could not trust her own judgment, not when it was clouded by foolish sentimentality.

Though her mother was flighty and often crass, Mary trusted that she wanted the best for all of her daughters. And in a rather roundabout way, she had successfully predicted matches between the two eldest girls with the richest gentlemen in the county. Lizzie and Jane were happy.

Mary would simply bow to her mother's decision, for it was far easier than making one of her own.

"Indeed, I do," Mrs. Bennet said, squeezing her daughter's arm gently.

"Then, I shall do my best to win him."

And to forget Mr. Hardcastle and her foolish heart's traitorous longing for him.

୬ଔ Nine ஒ๑

The drive to Mrs. Philips's house for the dinner party seemed shorter than usual. Dusk washed the world in muted tones, and even the dirty streets of Meryton took on a lovely somber appearance. Shops that had bustled with life hours earlier were now shut up tight, and the street vendors had returned to their places, wherever they might be.

The Philipses' home, lit with the glow of candlelight, provided a beacon that drew the Bennets' carriage onward, and soon, Mary and her parents were within the walls of the familiar dwelling.

Only it was not so familiar now. Candle flames danced on tabletops and wall sconces, and perhaps a dozen people filled the small, cluttered space. Mary wondered that they could all draw breath properly. She had expected a more intimate party, but in the confines of the chamber, the group appeared very large indeed.

"Has she invited the whole town?" Mary whispered to her mother.

"I do believe she has!" Mrs. Bennet trilled, merrily pulling her daughter into the largest group of people in the drawing room.

"It is all too much for me," Mr. Bennet said, deadpan. Then he faced Mary and offered her a gentle smile. "Remember what I told you, my dear. Choose wisely."

He straightened and looked about the room with vague disgust. "Now, I must seek out your uncle's good wine."

"Oh, Mr. Bennet!" his wife said. "You cannot leave us."

Finding that her husband had already retreated, Mrs. Bennet spoke again to Mary, her mind already back on her goals. "This is a fine way for you to make your entrance to the marriage mart. So many rich young men...and there is your prize!"

Mary stopped cold and looked in the direction her mother indicated.

Mr. George Randall stood beside his father. The younger was of average stature, though his mass of curly blond hair made him appear taller. He looked gentlemanly enough: handsome, well dressed, and well coiffed. He spoke with Mr. and Mrs. Philips whilst his father, Mr. John Randall, loomed behind him. The elder Randall was stern and stoic, two traits of which Mary heartily approved. She looked again to the son, her intended if Mrs. Bennet had her way. The sight of him drew no particular feeling from Mary.

Relieved, Mary smiled at her mother.

"You see! I knew you would approve of my selection," Mrs. Bennet whispered, having misinterpreted Mary's smile. "Let us meet your future husband."

Dragging Mary behind, Mrs. Bennet nudged her way toward Mrs. Philips.

With each step, Mary's feet turned increasingly leaden. Her mother's intentions must be clear to anyone who observed their movements.

Mary surveyed the room and was cowed by the realization that she and her mother held the focus of the entire party. Though every guest feigned disinterest, they all continued to cast them sidelong glances.

They knew what Mrs. Bennet was about.

Of course, this would be the case. Her mother had trumpeted the news of Mary's dowry in the streets of Meryton, so everyone knew this gathering was meant to dispose of that money—and Mary herself—to one fortunate gentleman.

Determined to ignore her feelings of embarrassment, Mary raised her chin slightly higher. And there, standing taller than the rest of the crowd, was Mr. Hardcastle. The unsteady candlelight cast quavering shadows across his sharp features. He did not play at coy, sidelong glances. No, his gaze was fastened upon Mary Bennet, and then he smiled with a mixture of understanding and amusement.

He empathized with her embarrassment. After all, his sister was just as confirmed a matchmaker as Mrs. Bennet. He understood.

Mary's heart fluttered, and joy washed through her.

Immediately, she chastised herself.

Resolved as she was to ignore her feelings and obey her practical mind, she ought not care that Mr. Hardcastle had come or that he understood her feelings. She should not notice how he seemed to see into her very soul from across the room. She should not feel anything at all for him.

She was here to win Mr. Randall. He was the practical choice. He would please her family. He would gain her a large estate and library.

Mary tore her gaze away from Mr. Hardcastle and vowed to avoid him for the duration of the evening if she possibly could.

She pinned her focus to her mother, who had managed to set them up at a proper distance from Mrs. Philips and waited for their hostess to invite them to join their conversation with the Randalls.

"Ah," Mrs. Philips said, opening the circle to include Mrs. Bennet and Mary. "Here is Miss Bennet now."

Mrs. Bennet pushed Mary forward and the introductions were made.

The gentlemen bowed, the ladies curtsied, and the youngest of the group studied each other while pretending not to be so engaged.

Now that she could look upon Mr. Randall more closely, she found that he was a well-looking gentleman. His dark eyes were serious, and to Mary's great relief, they did not elicit any sort of feeling within her heart.

Lack of feeling was a comfort.

Mary shifted her feet, wondering what she ought to say, but Mrs. Bennet found her voice first. Much to Mary's dismay, her mother addressed the elder Mr. Randall with a good deal too much flippancy in her voice. "Oh, Mr. Randall, we are ever so grateful that you have joined our little party tonight."

Mr. Randall made a grunting sound in the back of his throat. "Yes, well, it is the sort of evening that must be endured."

"Endured? What a good joke!" Mrs. Bennet said, giggling. "An evening in *our* company is not something that must be endured. Is not that true, Mary?"

Mary offered a half-hearted smile at the elder Mr. Randall, who only grunted again.

"Miss Bennet," the younger Mr. Randall said, abruptly taking a step nearer to Mary and blocking off her view of his father. "I hope you will allow me to escort you to dinner."

Mary regarded the gentleman. He seemed just as eager to end the awkward exchange as she was. And the only method for halting the contact between Mr. Randall and Mrs. Bennet was to assure both parents that the match was well underway.

"Thank you, sir," she said, giving him a conspiratorial smile. "It is very kind of you to offer."

"Then let us go in to dinner even now!" Mrs. Philips announced, as if waiting one more moment might undo the match. Waving her arms, she shepherded the whole party through the sea of furniture and toward the dining room.

⁓ Ten ⁓

Mary entered the dining room on Mr. Randall's arm and flushed at the sight she beheld. Even if her mother and aunt had not already published their intentions for the evening, one look around the table made their machinations obvious. The party was unequal in the number of ladies and gentlemen, and the latter group included only the most desired suitors in the county.

Mary did not know how to feel. While she was pleased to be on the favorable side of the ratio, she wished, as always, that her family had behaved more subtly.

And yet, she could not disappoint them.

Of the potential suitors at the table, only one among them mattered.

Mr. Randall sat across from her, studying his place setting.

Mary must make the most of her opportunity to snare him, but she must let him take the lead.

So she waited.

Through the entire first course, Mr. Randall remained obstinately silent.

Finally, Mary could manage the muteness no longer.

She asked the first socially acceptable question that came to mind: "How do you find the weather, Mr. Randall?"

The young man looked at her for the first time during the meal and said, "Agreeable."

"Yes," Mary said, smiling vapidly. "I find warm weather ever so agreeable. It makes for fine conditions on the roads."

"Indeed," Mr. Randall said. "We endured very few ruts on our journey here."

"I do not care for ruts either," Mary said.

In the space of half a minute, she and Mr. Randall had covered all the recommended topics of polite conversation.

She glanced down the length of the table and saw her mother eyeing her with frantic encouragement. Across from her, Mr. Bennet merely shrugged. She purposely did not look at Mr. Hardcastle or his sister.

Mary must hold further conversation with Mr. Randall, or her mother would intervene. She could not allow that to occur. She must converse on her own terms.

"Do you read, Mr. Randall?" she asked, promising herself that she would not utter one quotation, no matter what he read.

"Yes, I read," Mr. Randall said, his voice animated for the first time since they had been introduced.

"And what do you read?" Mary asked, pleased to have found a topic that might draw him out.

"Poetry," he said, smiling and leaning slightly forward in interest. "I confess to consuming a good deal of verse. Do you enjoy poetry, Miss Bennet?"

"Of course," Mary said. "Poetry was part of my education. Which poets do you admire?"

"Cowper, Byron...." His voice trailed off, and his expression turned misty.

For her own part, Mary did not look kindly upon these newest poets, finding their overt melodrama far too romantical for her own tastes. She wanted to say as much, and the words rushed to her lips. Alas, she could not very well speak such an opinion to Mr. Randall, who clearly adored them.

Mr. Randall's smile fell away, and his eyes remained wistful as he recited,

> Resigning every thought of bliss,
> Forever, from your love I go,
> Reckless of all the tears that flow,
> Disdaining thy polluted kiss.

Mary was acquainted enough with the work of Byron to know that the poem was titled "To Mary."

It must be a message.

Mr. Randall meant to court her.

After he completed his impassioned recitation, he looked at Mary with tired, earnest eyes. And she felt…nothing. Her heart did not leap, nor did her cheeks flush.

But her mind congratulated her. Mary Bennet had won the approval of a tolerably educated gentleman. Her parents would undoubtedly be pleased, and she would have to suffer none of the discomforts of feelings at all.

"What say you to this business with Napoleon, Mr. Randall?"

These words from Mary's uncle ripped her mind from its thoughts, and her head shot up in alarm.

She looked quickly at Mr. Randall to find the fervent sincerity drained from his features, and his gaze now returned to his plate.

Mary cast surprised eyes on Mr. Philips, wondering what he could be thinking to bring up such a topic at dinner, much less to Mr. Randall, whose mother hailed from France.

Mr. Randall fidgeted with the previously forgotten dining utensils and said, "I prefer to turn my mind to pleasanter matters."

Mary smiled at him with sympathetic approval. He had declined to comment with politeness, but her uncle would not allow it.

"Oh, come! You must have an opinion," Mr. Philips prodded.

Mary's eyes slid closed. Why would he not leave the subject? Did he not realize the awkward position in which he put his guest?

Slowly, Mary opened her eyes and met Mr. Randall's gaze again. He pressed his lips together in mute discomfort, and she knew what she must do.

Mary must prevent her uncle from delving further into such a forbidden topic. Rarely was she required to perform a conversational rescue, and recalling her mother's injunction against moralizing, she searched her mind for the proper method. She did not want to risk her potential union with Mr. Randall while attempting to save him.

Then, she thought of Miss Hardcastle's use of her femininity.

"Uncle," she said, voice quavering, "I believe Mr. Randall endeavors to protect me from such a disagreeable subject at dinner."

It was a lie, of course. Mary would have gladly listened to the bloodiest of war stories if it had not brought Mr. Randall such obvious distress.

"Oh yes, Mary," her uncle said, eyebrows upraised in surprise. "I had quite forgotten you were there. How very uncouth of me to broach such a subject in the presence of a lady."

Mary's spine prickled with annoyance at the idea that she might be incapable of overhearing a rational discussion of politics over a meal, but she also felt rather proud of her small deception. She glanced down the length of the table to where Miss Hardcastle sat with her brother.

Miss Hardcastle boasted of her ability to use her beauty and femininity to accomplish her will, and Mary too had employed that tactic this very night.

Perhaps she had not performed according to Miss Hardcastle's standards, but Mary Bennet had used her femininity to her advantage for the first time. It was all nonsense, of course—feigning distaste for serious talk—but her ploy had worked. She had used her womanly charms to save Mr. Randall from uneasiness.

This thought drew a smile to Mary's lips, and she turned her attention back to Mr. Randall, who offered her a small smile of admiration.

৩৩ Eleven ৩৬

After dinner, the ladies repaired to the drawing room while the gentlemen drank port and discussed topics unsuited for the ladies' hearing, probably the Napoleonic Wars.

When at last the gentlemen rejoined them, Mary found herself in the very position she had sought to avoid.

Before her stood Mr. Hardcastle.

Though a dozen people crowded the room, Mary and Mr. Hardcastle were separated from the group by an unfortunate cluster of her aunt's furniture. As such, they stood at rather a good distance from everyone else.

Despite the crowd, they were essentially alone.

Mr. Hardcastle watched her with such openness that Mary forgot her decision to avoid him at all costs. Instead, she curtsied, inviting the conversation.

Mr. Hardcastle bowed deeply, giving her a view of his short brown hair. Mary felt the oddest desire to touch the neat locks and determine if they were as soft as they appeared. Instead, she clutched her hands in front of her skirt.

"Good evening, Miss Bennet," he said, his soft voice sounding far more intimate than it ought.

"Good evening," Mary replied.

Mr. Hardcastle cast an amused glance about the room before returning his focus to Mary.

"If my senses do not deceive me, I believe your mother disapproves of your choice of conversation partner."

Mary looked over her shoulder to find her mother glowering at her. Upon gaining her daughter's noticed, Mrs. Bennet lifted her eyebrows and jerked her head toward Mr. Randall. Beside her, Mr. Bennet merely sipped his port.

Mary groaned and turned back to Mr. Hardcastle, her cheeks flaming at her mother's obvious display. This time, she could not quite meet his eye.

Mr. Hardcastle closed the distance between them ever so slightly, and when he leaned down to speak more privately, Mary looked up at him.

"'When a girl ceases to blush, she has lost the most powerful charm of beauty,'" he quoted softly.

Mary's brow furrowed at his words.

"For a gentleman who claims to see the merits of boldness in a female, I find it odd that you quote from Dr. Gregory. That passage, I believe, lists the merits of feminine reserve."

Mr. Hardcastle smiled fully upon her. "Indeed, I do not agree with the writer's every treatise, but it does not necessarily follow that I must discount him entirely. A flushed cheek enhances the beauty of the frank as well as the coy."

Preparing to dispute him, Mary parted her lips, but instead of speaking, she drew in a sharp breath. Was Mr. Hardcastle calling her—Mary, the plainest of all the Bennet sisters—beautiful?

"Though the pink in your cheeks is quite flattering," Mr. Hardcastle continued, his voice almost inaudible. His gaze slid momentarily in the direction of her mother. "I regret that this evening's purpose has put it there."

Confused, Mary let out a little breath. *This evening's purpose?*

He referred to her family's obvious intent to marry her off to Mr. Randall.

That thought jolted Mary back into reality, and she steeled herself. Her feelings for Mr. Hardcastle would gain her nothing but shame, and she must suppress them.

With a last look at his ardent face, Mary stepped backward, her slippers whispering across the floor until she felt her skirt brush one of the little tables that surrounded them, trapped them.

"Yes, my circumstances are quite different now," Mary said in a rush of breath.

She knew he took her meaning. He was aware of her mother and aunt's previous attempt to make a match between them, and he clearly comprehended that Mr. Randall was now the prize they sought.

Mr. Hardcastle raised his eyebrows, and he appeared to restrain himself from closing the distance between them again. "I—"

"I—I must not disappoint my mother," Mary blurted. She attempted to take another step back, but the small table prevented her from moving far. "I must not."

Mr. Hardcastle pressed his lips together and lowered his head. "I wish," he said quietly, "you might seek to gratify yourself and not your mother."

Panicked at the very idea, Mary held up a hand as if to ward off his suggestion.

"No," she said. "I must do what is expected of me…what is right."

Mr. Hardcastle raised his head, and what she saw was temptation itself. His eyes were wide, vulnerable, and slightly sad. She wanted to reach out, brush away his sorrow. She wanted to comfort him and herself as well.

"Dear Lord," Mary whispered to herself. She must flee from him immediately.

It seems that Mr. Hardcastle read her thoughts in her face, for he took a step forward.

She could not let him speak, must not allow him to convince her, to manipulate her feelings.

Mary burst out with a too loud "I must return to my mother. Pray, excuse me."

But she did not move.

In keeping with her proclamation that she must excuse herself, Mr. Hardcastle bowed, but his face remained upturned, giving Mary a chance to read the disappointment in his expression. A lump formed in her throat.

"You have set your course then," Mr. Hardcastle said.

Mary's mind worked sluggishly, and yet thoughts assailed her. This conversation was entirely too intimate for a dinner party. "You are very blunt, sir."

"And you are very coy," he said.

"I am not coy," Mary protested. "I do not hide who I am. I merely seek to do what is right."

Instead of curtsying as protocol demanded, she turned, narrowly avoided the infernal furnishings, and fled.

ᵒᵉ ᵉᵒ

Mary must have a moment to herself, a few minutes of peace so that she might think clearly.

She slipped out the drawing room door and into the empty foyer.

It was cooler and quieter in the hall. With the door to the drawing room closed, the sounds of the party faded into the background. No candles burned, leaving the hallway in almost pitch darkness.

Mary paced a few steps, stopping beside a longcase clock. She leaned against the wall and wondered what was wrong with her.

Why did she care what Mr. Hardcastle thought of her? His thoughts and opinions signified nothing. Why did she mind if he felt disappointment?

She ought not mind, but she did, very much.

Her attraction to Mr. Hardcastle was insupportable. It revealed a weakness of mind of which Mary had not believed herself capable. If she were not very careful indeed, this feeling would quite carry her away, and she would make a poor match.

It would be unthinkable to marry a law clerk when a landed gentleman sought her hand.

A common interest in quotations was not a foundation on which to build a marriage.

She must do as her family willed and marry for more practical reasons.

If only Mr. Hardcastle were other than what he was, if only he were not a law clerk, if only he were rich....

Mary shook the thoughts away, and the muted sounds of conversation returned to her consciousness. She must return to the party before her mother discovered her absence and sought her out. She could not bear her mother's chastisements at the moment.

She pushed away from the wall, but before she could take a step, the drawing room door opened. Mary heard Miss Hardcastle's sharp whisper.

"Simon! We must not leave now. It will be considered quite rude, and what will Mary say?"

Either Mr. Hardcastle did not respond or he did so in too quiet a tone for Mary to hear. She drew back behind the tall clock cabinet and listened.

"It is clear that there is a depth of sentiment between the two of you," Miss Hardcastle said, her voice a mixture of protest and confusion. "Why would you disappoint her by departing now? I believed you liked her."

Mary strained to hear Mr. Hardcastle's murmured response. "I do like her."

Mary's foolish pulse leapt with excitement and something like desire, but she tamped down her emotions.

"Then I demand an explanation," Miss Hardcastle said. "Why must we depart so suddenly?"

When Mr. Hardcastle spoke again, he sounded tired. "Did you not observe the guests, Pen? Read her mother's intent. It is plain as the lace on her dress. This is not merely a dinner party. This is a matchmaking scheme."

"You did not object to Mrs. Bennet's previous matchmaking scheme...when you were the beneficiary."

"Well," Mr. Hardcastle said with resignation in his voice, "Miss Bennet made it clear that her circumstances are changed."

"But she feels for you," Miss Hardcastle protested.

"I hoped it was so," Mr. Hardcastle said, voice turning wistful, "but she will not allow it. She fears her feelings, mistrusts them."

Though Mary could not see the Hardcastle siblings from her place against the wall, she imagined that Miss Hardcastle looked upon her brother with pity.

"I am sorry, Simon, but perhaps this is for the best. Much as I like Miss Bennet, I do not wish to see you suffer as the husband of a woman who does not know her own mind."

Mary's forehead creased.

What was Miss Hardcastle talking of? Mary knew her own mind!

She had spent her entire life as a student of the mind. She relished study and contemplation, and her reading had taught her that feelings were untrustworthy. She must let reason be her guide. And reason told her that her parents were correct: a woman must marry for security, not love.

"However," Miss Hardcastle said, her voice thoughtful, "you have held but a few conversations with her. Perhaps she is not yet comfortable allowing her feelings to guide her. Perhaps all that is required is time."

"I am not in control of the time available," Mr. Hardcastle said simply.

"No, I grant you," Miss Hardcastle agreed. "Her mother is in great haste to see her married." She paused and added, "If only Mary were not so determined to hold to errant teachings on restraint and modesty that she denied her own heart…such a foolish notion indeed! Perhaps her mind may be changed.…"

"Pen," Mr. Hardcastle said with affectionate exasperation. "Your faith in Miss Bennet does you credit, but I fear this shall not end well."

Any reply Miss Hardcastle might have offered was overwhelmed by Mrs. Bennet's voice as she screeched into the hall.

"Mary!"

Mrs. Bennet burst into the center of the Hardcastles' private conversation without an apology.

Mary's pulse quickened. She would certainly be caught eavesdropping.

"Have you seen Mary? She is needed at the pianoforte."

"No," Miss Hardcastle said, her voice calm. "We stepped into the foyer to get some air and have not encountered her here."

"Well, then I must go and find her. The two of you must take your seats, or you shall miss her performance."

With that, Mrs. Bennet shoved the Hardcastle siblings back into the drawing room, unknowingly saving Mary from much embarrassment at being discovered.

Nothing Mrs. Bennet could do, however, would save Mary from what she had overheard.

Miss Hardcastle's proclamation stung, and moreover, it was utterly incorrect.

Mary knew her own mind, and her every decision reflected that fact.

She clenched her hands. In matters of matrimony, a wise woman allows herself to be guided by logic and reason. Giving way to feelings creates nothing but strife.

Had Mary not witnessed the phenomenon herself? And had she not also witnessed the exact opposite?

She covered her eyes with a shaking hand and turned the matter over in her mind. Alas, she could not reconcile Lydia's romantic disaster with the love matches her sisters Jane and Lizzie had made.

Only one thing could be concluded with certainty: Lydia had displayed a careless disregard for propriety. Mary could not allow herself to behave with such indiscretion.

She must be cautious and hold firm to her purpose.

Mary could not allow her mind to be swayed by anything, not her own emotions and certainly not the pert opinions of the Hardcastles. She would not abandon the moral precepts she had learned. She would not disappoint her parents.

And she would certainly not think upon Mr. Hardcastle again!

"Mary!" Mrs. Bennet called again.

Startled from her ruminations, Mary dropped her hand and dared a peek around the clock.

"Oh! Where has that girl gotten to?" Mrs. Bennet demanded as she marched in the opposite direction.

Mary stepped from behind the clock and sneaked back into the drawing room. Unfortunately, her reentry did not go unnoticed.

Mrs. Philips spotted her immediately, approached, and then gave her a heavy nudge in the direction of the pianoforte. "I believe it is time for some music. Your mother has been in search of you."

"I am sorry, Aunt. I required only a moment to gather myself. I am ready now."

Those last words were spoken to convince herself, but they fell flat.

Still, the purpose of the evening was to show herself to her advantage and thereby woo Mr. Randall. She must do her best to display her accomplishments and forget what she had heard in the hallway.

She looked quickly to her father who stood nearby.

He nodded and gave her an understanding smile. "This is your night, my dear."

As if in a dream—or perhaps a nightmare—Mary floated to the pianoforte.

Usually, she exploited every opportunity to perform, but now, she wanted the formality over so she could think about what she had heard.

Mary felt her own artifice keenly as she settled on the stool, adjusted her wrinkled skirt, and opened the music she had chosen for the evening: one of her favorite concertos.

Settling her fingers on the appropriate keys, she became aware of every movement, cough, and whisper in the room.

Without a glance at the music, Mary began to play, but her heart was not in it.

৯৫ Twelve ৯৯

A gentleman in pursuit of a lady with a large dowry does not hesitate.

Mary discovered this truth the morning after the Philipses' dinner party. She had passed an ill night of little sleep. She got out of bed long after the sun rose, feeling tired and cross, and joined her parents for a late breakfast.

Mary sat at the table with her hands wrapped around her teacup. The warm china heated her fingers, and the strong tea warmed her from the inside. But it was not enough to unknot her stomach or thaw the coldness around her heart.

Logic told Mary that she had no reason for such a glum countenance, but her heart refused to listen.

A knock sounded at the door, and Mary barely lifted her head when Hill entered bearing a letter for Mr. Bennet.

"This came for you, sir," she said.

Mrs. Bennet squealed, a sound that made Mary's head pound harder, and snatched the paper before her father could reach for it. Mary put down her teacup and rubbed her temples.

"You see, Mary! What did I tell you? An offer has arrived," she cried, waving it about for all to see.

Mr. Bennet rose from the table, a piece of toast in his hand, and beat a hasty retreat.

His wife turned to call after him. "Mr. Bennet, do not forsake us! This letter is addressed to you, my dear. We require your opinion on this matter."

Mr. Bennet scarcely paused in his flight. "I do not recall a time when my opinion was heeded, my dear. Simply alert me to Mary's choice, and I shall give my consent."

"An offer?" Mary asked, her stomach tightening again. "I do not believe myself prepared to receive an offer of marriage."

Mary frowned at her own words. Spoken aloud, it almost sounded as if Miss Hardcastle had been right in her assessment the night before.

It sounded very much like she did not know her own mind.

But it was the truth. Mary did not know if she was ready for this offer.

Confused, she dropped her face into her hands.

"Pish!" Mrs. Bennet cried as she eagerly broke the seal and searched for the name of the sender. "Mr. Randall has proposed just as I predicted!"

Mary lifted her head and stared at her mother.

Mrs. Bennet shook the paper at Mary. "How very traditional and formal he is! A letter such as this is the mark of an excellent gentleman."

Mary reached for it, but Mrs. Bennet refused to relinquish it.

"Let me see," she murmured before scanning the bulk of the correspondence. "He makes some comments on your beauty, your conversation...your act of salvation?"

Surprise pulled a grin to Mary's reluctant lips.

"What does that mean?" Mrs. Bennet demanded.

"I prevented him from enduring an unpleasant conversation."

"Well, it is a morning for joyful surprises," Mrs. Bennet said, returning to her reading. "Here! Listen to what he says. 'It is the fondest wish of my father that we might unite our houses.' What say you, Mary?"

Mary blinked. "He truly wishes to make an offer?"

"Indeed! Look. Here is a portion regarding the settlement!" She waved the paper vaguely in her daughter's direction again, but did not let her see it closely. "Oh, Mary! You shall have Ashworth, and all you must give in exchange is Mr. Darcy's dowry. You are the victor in this marriage, my girl. You shall ascend to the apex of Meryton society! It is all I have ever dreamed of!"

From here, Mrs. Bennet's conversation devolved into high-pitched squeals, and Mary could bear the delight no longer. She forced the letter from her mother's fingertips and left the table.

She must find a quiet place to think. She walked slowly to the empty sitting room and read the contents of the letter twice.

For a gentleman who professed to love the poetry of Byron, Mr. Randall's letter rather resembled business correspondence, including a section regarding the particulars of the marriage settlement.

Mary put the letter aside. Never having been one to consult her feelings over her judgment, she realized that both faculties were equally discomfited by Mr. Randall's proposal. However, she could not justify her reaction, for this was precisely the path she was determined to pursue.

This proposal was the desired result.

Based on her overjoyed peals of laughter, Mrs. Bennet had no second thoughts.

Mr. Bennet would also be pleased, for the settlement sounded equitable. And who could object to a daughter's ascension to one of the finest houses in the county?

For her own part, Mary ought to be well satisfied with the situation. The library alone should have been adequate inducement.

All facets taken into consideration, a union with Mr. Randall was far from objectionable. All her criteria had been met, and yet Mary's unease persisted.

"What do you say, Mary?" Mrs. Bennet asked from the doorway of the sitting room some minutes later. "Are you pleased to become Mr. Randall's wife?"

That was, indeed, a good question.

Marrying Mr. Randall was the correct action for a young lady of Mary's age and status. He was a gentleman from a well-respected family with a large estate.

Not only was it right, but it was the course of action she had already chosen. She could not allow herself to deviate from her plan, no matter how tempted she felt.

"Well?" Mrs. Bennet prodded. "Speak, Child!"

Mary's breath hitched in her throat, but she managed to say, "I suppose I shall be pleased to accept his offer of marriage."

·ଓଡ଼ Thirteen ଓଡ଼·

Upon Mary's acceptance of Mr. Randall's proposal, the Randalls and the Bennets negotiated the terms of the marriage settlement through their attorneys. Mr. Randall retained the services of an attorney in London, and the Bennets, of course, trusted their affairs to Mr. Philips.

Soon, all that remained was for Mr. Bennet to sign the documents that would transfer Mary's newfound wealth to her future husband.

The legal matters quickly got underway, leaving Mary rather adrift. One moment, she felt nothing but determination to marry Mr. Randall, and the next, she desired only to beg her father to call off the engagement.

Because there was no one with whom Mary might discuss her confusion, she remained silent on the subject.

Meanwhile, her mother was not so silent. She spoke endlessly of wedding preparations—gowns, flowers, ribbons, and cakes—leaving Mary to conclude that it was already too late to change her mind. Even now, Mrs. Bennet busied herself in Mary's bedchamber. All her gowns were laid out for inspection.

Mary's opinions had not been required, so she took herself to the sitting room.

"Mary must have at least three new gowns, Hill," Mrs. Bennet proclaimed, her voice carrying down the stairs to Mary's ears. "Perhaps four. She cannot go to Ashworth wearing these drab frocks. If she is to be mistress of the house, she must shine!"

Mary's mind continued to wander in inappropriate directions. It would be better for her to keep herself busy with a task, but she absolutely refused to go to her mother and help destroy her wardrobe.

A knock sounded at the front door, and Mary's head shot up in surprise.

Grateful for the distraction, she hurried to the door, the tap of her boots on the wood floors barely audible under the sound of her mother's voice.

"Imagine it, Hill. Our little Mary shall be the wife of Mr. George Randall and mistress of Ashworth."

Mary sighed as she grasped the cool metal knob in her palm. She pulled open the door and barely restrained a horrified gasp.

"Mr. Hardcastle!" she cried far louder than she should have into a suddenly silent house.

"Who said anything about Mr. Hardcastle?" Mrs. Bennet called from above stairs. "Your uncle quite admires him, but he is nothing but a tradesman. You are above him, Mary."

Mary's fingers tightened convulsively on the knob, and she had the sudden impulse to slam the door. She certainly could not face Mr. Hardcastle.

First, she had invited him to a dinner party where she was courted by another gentleman.

Then, his sister insulted Mary's mental fortitude.

Now, her mother insulted him.

And worst of all, he stood there, smiling at her in amusement. She lowered her gaze.

"I—I—" Mary stammered, staring at the tips of his boots. "I do apologize, sir, for, well…."

Mr. Hardcastle's laugh rang out, and Mary looked up.

"You laugh?" Mary asked, incredulous.

"Of the possible responses," Mr. Hardcastle said, still chuckling lightly, "I find it the best option." He sobered. "Furthermore, your mother speaks the truth. I am a law clerk, and you are a gentleman's daughter. I cannot dispute her."

He left the obvious unsaid. According to societal wisdom, Mary was indeed above him, with or without Mr. Darcy's dowry.

Mary nearly gave in to the temptation to remind Mr. Hardcastle that her mother's own family sustained itself in the legal trade, but any such comment seemed to offer unjust hope. She could not make that mistake a second time.

"It would be very hypocritical of me to think ill of your mother's truth-telling after I proclaimed my admiration for honesty." Mr. Hardcastle patted the leather saddlebag he held. "In addition, it would make my errand here far more awkward."

"What is your errand, Mr. Hardcastle?" Mary asked.

"Your uncle has sent me to deliver papers for your father to sign."

The marriage settlement.

Her uncle had sent Mr. Hardcastle to assist in her engagement to another man.

Mary shuddered and wondered what her uncle could possibly be thinking. He knew of his wife's aborted attempt to match them. Why would he send Mr. Hardcastle?

"Oh dear," Mary said with a small groan. She reached out a hand. "I mean to say…shall I take the documents to my father?"

Mr. Hardcastle kept the bag in his grasp. "I fear my errand is to witness his signing and then return the papers to Mr. Philips."

Mary wondered how matters could worsen, and then she answered the question herself.

"Well, if you can bear my mother," Mary blurted, "and you must deliver the papers to my father personally, then do come inside."

Mr. Hardcastle chuckled. "I find your mother very agreeable. She speaks her mind."

"Yes," Mary agreed. "Too often and too loudly."

Mary led Mr. Hardcastle toward her father's private chamber.

"I am informed that I must offer you my felicitations on your engagement, Miss Bennet."

"You are *informed* that you must do so?" Mary repeated, pausing midstride and turning to him.

Mr. Hardcastle raised an eyebrow. "I am required to make my congratulations, am I not?"

"I suppose," Mary said, dissecting his words. Mr. Hardcastle was careful with his diction. "But why do you say you are 'required' to do so?"

"Your acquaintances must offer their best wishes." His tone was bland, but his eyes were bright. "We are friends, are we not?"

Now, Mary studied him. His expression told her quite clearly that his tone was deceptively mild.

"Yes, we are friends," Mary said. "But your phrasing…you do not truly wish the best for me?"

"Absolutely, I do," Mr. Hardcastle replied quickly, but he said nothing more.

Mary frowned and tried to concentrate on deciphering his meaning. "Then, you question my decision."

Mr. Hardcastle's gaze intensified. "It would be impolitic of me to confirm your assertion," he said. "Especially given the fact that my errand is to seal your marriage settlement."

Her jaw clenched. Indeed, Mr. Hardcastle had no right to question her decision. It was her choice to marry Mr. Randall, and she had been motivated by reason and wisdom, not love and romance. She must stay her course.

She turned and rapped at her father's door. "Papa, Mr. Hardcastle is here to see you."

"Enter," Mr. Bennet said from behind the closed door.

Mary did as he bade, and her father stood, bowing to Mr. Hardcastle. "Ah, Mr. Hardcastle. I have been expecting you."

Mary gave a brief curtsey and prepared to excuse herself.

"Mary," her father said, looking between his daughter and his guest with assessing eyes. "As this matter concerns you, I believe you ought to stay. Be seated, both of you."

"But—" Mary began her protest. She had no way of explaining the awkwardness of this situation to her father without increasing her own humiliation. "Ladies do not often take part in legal matters," she concluded.

"Let us break with convention, then," Mr. Bennet said.

Mr. Hardcastle smiled at Mary, perhaps as a method of apologizing to her, and then turned back to Mr. Bennet. He removed the papers from his satchel and passed them across the desk.

"The documents are in order, sir. All that is left is for you to sign them."

"The engagement will be complete, and Mary's dowry will legally belong to Mr. Randall." Mr. Bennet then studied the papers in silence for a moment. "If you will excuse me, I will go somewhere quiet to review these."

Mary's stomach dropped. Her father would not leave her in a room alone with a gentleman!

"Papa?" she squeaked.

"Entertain Mr. Hardcastle for a few moments. I shall return in due course."

He did not allow time for Mary to object. He simply walked from the room, leaving the door open behind him.

Silence settled around Mary and Mr. Hardcastle.

After long moments, Mr. Hardcastle said, "I suppose we must speak."

"It is the accepted convention," Mary admitted, feeling tired and out of sorts. "But please, let us not discuss the roads or weather."

"That certainly limits my selection of topics," Mr. Hardcastle said wryly. He pretended to ponder his next words, eliciting a small laugh from Mary.

Finally, he said, "My sister tells me that there is soon to be a ball."

"Yes," Mary said, feeling comfortable with the topic. He referred to Meryton's public ball. "It is a yearly event. Everyone awaits it with eager anticipation."

Everyone except Mary. Balls and dancing did not entice her.

"Penelope requires me to attend," he said, affection for his sister evident in his tone. "She does enjoy a ball."

"She would get along well with my sisters then. They love to dance."

"But you do not care to dance?" Mr. Hardcastle asked.

Mary shook her head. "It is not so much that I do not care to dance, but I have not often had the opportunity of joining in."

"Why ever not?"

"At a small assembly, someone is required to provide the music so that others might dance, and my sisters always insisted that I should be the provider."

"And at a large assembly?"

"I have never thought much of dancing," Mary hedged, realizing too late that she had just proclaimed the opposite. The truth of the matter was that if Mary was not at her place behind the pianoforte, then she always seemed to want for partners.

"I confess I did not at first comprehend the attraction," he said companionably. "But one cannot be related to Penelope without being forced to learn to dance. She assured me there was more to dancing than organized movement about the floor. She was correct."

"Was she?" Mary murmured, not realizing she had spoken her thought aloud. She had never quite experienced the attraction herself. Perhaps it was the simple act of getting nearer to a gentleman.

Mary's eyes slid to Mr. Hardcastle. He met her gaze steadily. She might not object to getting nearer to him.

Immediately, she blushed.

The tone of the room became somber. Mr. Hardcastle studied her.

"I suppose I shall see you dancing the night through with Mr. Randall."

Mary's cheeks reddened further, and she looked away. "It is improper for a woman to dance more than two dances with any gentleman, even her intended."

"Yes, of course, two dances only. Even with your intended," he said as if he had momentarily forgotten his purpose in calling upon Mr. Bennet.

Now it was his turn to look away.

A moment later, Mr. Bennet returned and took his place behind the desk.

He picked up his pen and held it over the paper.

"Well, Mary," he said. "By my signing this, your choice will have been made."

Mary's stomach plummeted. This was an irrevocable moment. Once her father signed those documents, Mary and her dowry would be forever linked with Mr. Randall.

She did not allow herself even a glance at Mr. Hardcastle.

"I know, Papa. I have given my word, and I must follow through."

"And you, Mr. Hardcastle, agree to serve as witness?"

"I do," he said, his voice sounding strained.

Mr. Bennet sighed, shook his head, and signed the papers. Thus, Mary's engagement to Mr. Randall became official.

❧ Fourteen ❧

Mrs. Bennet threw herself headlong into the wedding preparations, carrying Mary along with her.

Time passed quickly, and soon the night of the Meryton ball arrived. Mary had grown to anticipate the event, for it would be the first time she would see Mr. Randall since their engagement two weeks prior.

Such an odd thing, a public ball, Mary thought as she observed a group of girls dash by in a swirl of skirts and giggles. *Anyone from the highest to the lowest social orders might attend.*

Mrs. Bennet grasped Mary's hand, pulling her from her reverie and towing her across the ballroom toward a group of matrons and their unwed daughters.

"Have you heard our delightful news?" Mrs. Bennet called upon her approach. "Our Mary has made a most fortuitous match!"

Mrs. Bennet had already announced her daughter's engagement to all her acquaintances, but she continued to trumpet it nonetheless. As a result of her mother's unabashed boastfulness, Mary heard many repetitious felicitations. Beneath the good wishes, however, she detected envy and perhaps disdain.

Mary glanced about her, feeling suddenly overwhelmed by the sound and movement and expectation.

"Mama," said Mary softly in Mrs. Bennet's ear, "I must beg a few minutes of fresh air…."

Mrs. Bennet did not so much as incline her head toward her daughter. Instead, she looked alertly toward the far end of the ballroom. Mary followed her gaze and soon spied the object that drew her mother's attention.

Her fiancé approached.

"You have an abundance of air in this very room," Mrs. Bennet said carelessly. "Mr. Randall and his father approach even now. Do behave yourself."

Mary hardly heard her mother's instruction, for her focus was entirely on Mr. George Randall. He bowed, and she curtsied.

Mr. Randall's eyes remained downcast, offering her no reassurance at all. Mary, feeling even more ill at ease, transferred her focus to the floor beneath his booted feet.

Then, as if remembering his purpose, Mr. Randall stepped toward Mary. "Will you do me the honor of the first two dances, Miss Bennet?"

"Certainly, sir," she replied, experiencing the same discomfiture that she had felt at Aunt Philips's dinner party. Mr. Randall seemed so very unsettled, and she could not decide if the sensation emanated from his father, who loomed behind him, or some other source.

In due course, the first dance of the evening was called, and Mr. Randall escorted her to the floor for the opening set. The music called forth the required steps from Mary's feet, and for a time, she concentrated only on the dance without speaking. Mr. Randall too kept quiet.

Even during pauses in the dance, the couple remained silent, and Mary felt her uneasiness mount.

Finally, she could bear it no longer and asked, "Are you in good health this evening, Mr. Randall?"

"What?" he asked as though his mind had been otherwise engaged.

Mary repeated her question.

"Oh yes," he said, glancing about the room. "I am in good health. I thank you for the inquiry. And are you in good health?"

"Indeed, very good health, sir," Mary said, now studying him with care. She could not help thinking something was amiss, but she could not name it.

"I find I must apologize for my apparent unsociability," Mr. Randall said as the dance continued. "I am not the most adept partner and must concentrate on the steps so that I do not bring you embarrassment."

Mary studied his movements more carefully. He did not seem awkward on his feet. In fact, he maneuvered himself much more pleasingly than Mr. Collins at the Netherfield ball. True, Mr. Randall's steps occasionally faltered, but he had not yet trod on her slippers or crashed into another couple.

"How very thoughtful of you to consider my feelings in the matter," Mary said because it was the proper response. "But I believe you do not give yourself enough credit. You dance well. But truly, sir, you seem preoccupied this evening."

Mr. Randall's eyebrows raised in surprise, and Mary knew she had said too much. She wished immediately that she had adhered to banalities.

"No," Mr. Randall assured her, casting his gaze aside. "You are mistaken. I am only concentrating on the steps. That is all."

"I am pleased to hear it," Mary said, though she did not believe him.

When the dances ended, Mr. Randall returned her to her mother. After inquiring as to her comfort and then standing beside them for some time, he excused himself, leaving Mary confused and alone.

✒ ✒ ✒

An hour later, Miss Hardcastle appeared at Mary's elbow, nearly dislodging a glass of punch from her fingers.

"You must come with me this moment," she whispered, her tone full of urgency.

"Miss Hardcastle?" Mary said, feeling resentment rise within her. "What ever is the matter?"

Prepared to rebuke Miss Hardcastle, Mary set down her cup, turned, and saw that the young woman's sapphire eyes were clearly troubled.

"You must come even now!"

"Where must I come, and why?" Mary demanded.

"We have not the time for interrogation," Miss Hardcastle said, taking Mary's hand. "Come with me."

Mary sighed, allowing herself again to be pulled along toward she knew not what.

Miss Hardcastle bustled Mary across the crowded room to a spot near the balcony door.

"Now," Miss Hardcastle whispered in her ear, "we may observe from here, but no closer."

Mary furrowed her brows at Miss Hardcastle. "I do not comprehend…."

"Shhh! Observe and listen." Miss Hardcastle pointed toward a couple engaged in conversation.

"It is Mr. Randall," Mary said, surprised to find her fiancé with a woman. Was this an illicit rendezvous? She had read that such things occurred on balconies.

"My brother and I came upon them quite by accident. They were engaged in so deep a conversation that they hardly noticed us."

Mr. Randall and the young lady made an elegant picture, washed in the moonlight and shadow.

Even in the dimness of the evening, Mary could see that the young woman was clad in an ill-fitting gown. The fabric gaped alarmingly at the bosom, and a large ribbon cinched the generous bodice around her waist.

Despite her improperly tailored dress, the young lady was quite pretty. Moonlight sparkled on her dewy skin, highlighting an upturned nose and delicate mouth.

Mary narrowed her eyes in speculation.

Mr. Randall's shy bearing had given way to something else entirely. He had appeared reluctant during their dance. Now he appeared, well, desperate.

He clutched the woman's hand, and tension was alive between them.

"He appears *devoted* to her," Mary whispered, horrified. "I am engaged to him, and yet I scarcely know him at all."

Mary had believed she and Mr. Randall had made a match based on mutual existence and corresponding needs. It seemed rather simple to her, but perhaps she had oversimplified the situation.

Perhaps there was more to his story. Maybe he was not the gentleman she—and her family—had believed him to be. Would he take her dowry and use it to subsidize his mistress?

Did he love this woman?

He had quoted poetry to Mary not so long ago. Was not love of poetry the symptom of a romantic heart?

As if in answer to her unspoken question, Mr. Randall leaned down and kissed the young lady's knuckles.

Mary's breath came fast, and she felt suddenly faint. That was certainly not proper behavior for a newly engaged gentleman.

He *did* love the young lady.

What would Mary do now? Her engagement to Mr. Randall was official, but she could not wed him if he loved another, as he clearly did. And the dowry? It had already been signed over to him.

She turned wide eyes to Miss Hardcastle, who gave her a sorrowful look. "I am sorry. I thought you ought to see for yourself."

Without thinking, Mary said the first words that came to mind: "'And immediately there fell from his eyes as it had been scales: and he received sight forthwith, and arose.'"

Though Miss Hardcastle looked at Mary as if she had just grown scales herself, Mary drew great comfort from the words. Seeing the truth for the first time was indeed painful, and she felt a keen disappointment in herself for misjudging the situation. And yet, despite it all, her heart remained uninjured.

She pressed her lips together, determined to set matters to rights.

"This will not do," she said, though she had little hope of rectifying the matter now.

❦ Fifteen ❦

Despite the noise and the crush of humanity in the ballroom around her, Mary felt very much alone.

Standing just as Miss Hardcastle left her, Mary continued to study the couple on the balcony.

Of what might they be talking?

Out of sheer desperation, Mary edged closer, deciding her behavior could not possibly be described as eavesdropping. This was research, the gathering of additional information. She was not being rude. After all, they were conversing in public where anyone might overhear.

And she was engaged to Mr. Randall. She deserved to know the truth.

Mary slipped out the door to the balcony and edged closer to the party in question, pausing at various distances, trying to catch wind of their conversation without drawing too near.

Alas, she could hear nothing of Mr. Randall and the lady, and she could not move closer without making her presence known. Frustrated, Mary pondered the wisdom of simply joining them. Mr. Randall was *her* fiancé. She had a perfect right to approach him, did she not? She ought to go and seek an introduction, if not an explanation for his undue attention to her.

Mary steeled herself to join the couple, but when she finally stepped forward, she encountered the sudden view of a gentleman's waistcoat.

"I beg your pardon," Mary said before looking up and encountering the penetrating eyes of Mr. Hardcastle.

"Good evening, Miss Bennet," he said, seemingly oblivious to her intended path.

"Good evening, Mr. Hardcastle," she said, attempting to conceal her irritation even as she peeked around his tall frame to discover that Mr. Randall withdrew even now from his conversation with the mysterious woman.

Gritting her teeth, Mary glared at Mr. Hardcastle. He had caused her to miss the opportunity of discovering something of her betrothed's relationship with the young lady.

Mr. Hardcastle regarded her blandly.

"Would you care to dance?" he asked. "If you are not engaged for the next two dances...."

"You must be aware that I am, in fact, *engaged*," Mary began, allowing her frustration to seep into her speech, "to be married to Mr. Randall. It would be best if I did not confuse the issue by accepting the invitation of another gentleman."

Mr. Hardcastle glanced over his shoulder at the young lady Mr. Randall had just left.

"An engaged woman must limit her partners to her fiancé alone? I did not believe that to be the convention."

Mary glared at him. Mr. Hardcastle was infuriatingly correct. She was free to dance with any gentleman who asked her. Even engaged couples could not stand up together more than twice in one evening. Moreover, it was expected for them to serve as partners to other dancers.

But now was not the time for dancing. Now was the time to avert a disaster.

Unfortunately, Mary had not developed a repertoire of polite excuses, and with no pretext to offer, she must consent to dance with Mr. Hardcastle.

"Oh!" Mary said, reaching toward his proffered arm. "Let us be done with this."

Mr. Hardcastle grinned at her, took her hand, and placed it on his forearm. "Then, do come and dance with me. Listen, the music begins."

Mary watched him askance, wishing she could excuse herself, but she allowed him to lead her to the floor.

When her gloved hand slipped into Mr. Hardcastle's, and their eyes met, all thoughts of Mr. Randall and his young lady fled from her mind.

Mary's breath caught in her throat, and she nearly missed the opening steps of the dance. She felt her cheeks grow hot as she stumbled back into time with the music.

What is becoming of me? Am I no better than Mr. Collins?

Mary's heart constricted.

This was not how her life ought to be.

Mary Bennet behaved with sense, relying on reason alone to guide her decisions. She comported herself with a meekness that befit her sex. She honored her parents and God.

According to her studies, this conduct would yield a happy life. She would be safe and secure. She would have the respect of gentlemen and her society alike.

And yet her fiancé could barely force himself to complete two dances with Mary, and then, moments later, he kissed the hand of another woman.

That was not how it ought to be.

Worse, Mary danced in the arms of a gentleman who was not her intended, and she enjoyed it. Her heart raced, and her face flushed. Sensations skittered from the tips of her toes to the top of her head.

When the last chord sounded, Mary was surprised. She and her partner had completed two dances with barely a word spoken between them, and nary a quotation to be had.

Now, as he escorted her toward her mother, Mr. Hardcastle slowed his pace and leaned ever so slightly closer to her ear.

"Miss Bennet," he said softly, "do not forfeit your own happiness for any reason. My greatest desire is to see you truly happy."

Mary felt his breath whisper against her neck, causing that tingling sensation to descend her spine again.

She turned her wide eyes upon Mr. Hardcastle, and the other occupants of the ballroom seemed to vanish into a misty dream. Her steps halted of their own accord.

"I do not believe I shall ever be happy," Mary admitted.

"Do you not, Miss Bennet?" Mr. Hardcastle asked. "You deserve happiness, and you must do what is necessary to attain it."

Mary could not find the proper response.

"No matter what you choose," Mr. Hardcastle said, "I shall remain your friend."

"And I shall remain yours," Mary whispered, her voice hitching.

"You know where to find me," he said, "if you should require me."

Then, they were walking again, and Mary was delivered safely to her mother.

༝ଙ Sixteen ଙ༝

"Two partners in one evening!" Mrs. Bennet exclaimed after Mr. Hardcastle departed. "How very fortunate for you, Mary." She paused and considered her daughter for a quick moment. "You do look quite lovely, despite your hair. Your coloring is rather radiant in this light. I do believe your engagement agrees with you."

Mary felt herself flush again, for she knew that her high coloring resulted from her conversation with Mr. Hardcastle and not from her engagement to Mr. Randall. If anything, her color would turn wan upon thinking of Mr. Randall and his mystery woman.

She glanced over her shoulder to find the gentleman in question approaching from the opposite end of the room. She whirled back to Mrs. Bennet. Perhaps her mother's tactless nature could prove useful.

"Mama," Mary whispered, "will you arrange for Mr. Randall to call upon us?"

Mrs. Bennet clapped her hands with delight. "Why, of course, my dear! You are ever so in love with him, are you not? You cannot be without your betrothed for another day."

Squelching the temptation to demand that her mother lower her voice, Mary cringed and whispered, "It is only that I should like to speak privately with Mr. Randall."

Again, Mrs. Bennet misinterpreted her meaning. She giggled loudly. "You desire a romantic rendezvous before you marry. How delightful!"

"Mama!" Mary exclaimed, preparing to correct her. Then, her lips fell silent as she recalled her mother's reaction when Lizzie had rejected Mr. Collins's proposal. The memory of shrieked demands and claims of sick headaches returned to Mary with alarming clarity. With Mr. Randall approaching, she could not risk such a display.

Moreover, Mary realized she could not confide her fears in her mother at all, for the merest hint that her engagement to Mr. Randall was in danger would send Mrs. Bennet into a true panic. It was best for her to continue to believe that Mary's future was arranged to everyone's satisfaction.

But Mary's future had never been in greater peril.

The marriage settlement had already been drawn and signed, legally transferring ownership of all Mary's property, including Mr. Darcy's gift, to Mr. Randall. Mary could not so much as dispose of a gown without potential repercussions from the Randalls. Mr. Bennet had signed away both his money and Mr. Darcy's.

And monetary loss was not the only damage she might cause.

Reputations also would be shattered.

Attempting to end the engagement would lower Mary's place in society and destroy her only chance of gaining a husband in the future. Worse, rather than being seen as the respectable, accomplished young lady she dreamed of being, Mary Bennet would be viewed forever as a pariah, a jilt, a foolish girl who had squandered her one chance at happiness.

She would be no better than her silly sister Lydia.

Mary's shoulders slumped. She had only herself to blame. She had always wanted to be seen and appreciated for her accomplishments, and she had acted to please her parents and to raise herself in the esteem of the town by marrying Meryton's most sought-after bachelor. She had never considered the possibility that attaining her dream might bring her such potential for unhappiness.

Her mother's voice yanked Mary from her consternation.

"Oh! Mr. Randall," Mrs. Bennet enthused. She gave her daughter a stern look before turning back to the gentleman. "Do not mind my daughter. She was deep in thought about your wedding, I am sure."

"I—I," Mary stammered. "I was thinking of our future."

"You cut quite a dashing figure on the dance floor, Mr. Randall," Mrs. Bennet continued, oblivious to Mary's discomfort. "If you don't mind my saying so."

"You are all kindness," replied Mr. Randall, bowing to her slightly. "I fear you are too generous, for I am well aware of my flaws."

He glanced sidelong at Mary, and she thought she might have read guilt in the quick look.

"Well, we see no such flaws," Mrs. Bennet protested, looking to her daughter for support. "Do we, Mary?"

Burdened by the weight of her situation, Mary could not manage to compose a reply and fell back on what was comfortable. "We are told to 'judge not,' and so I shall keep silent on the matter."

"Mary!" her mother shrieked, dismayed by her daughter's implication.

Mr. Randall smiled crookedly at her. "What a kind way of agreeing with me, Miss Bennet. It is no secret that dancing is not among my greatest talents, as I have often been told."

Mary studied her would-be husband. He did not seem to be the sort of gentleman who would flaunt his unfaithfulness or steal a young woman's dowry. He seemed perfectly agreeable, even now. But that could not be.

"Do not listen to my daughter, sir," Mrs. Bennet said. "She is overtired from dancing, for she has never had so many partners in one evening. You must come and see her again after she has taken the opportunity of resting. Perhaps later in the week you would do us the honor of paying a visit to Longbourn."

Mr. Randall looked to Mary and smiled again.

"I would be most happy to call upon you, Miss Bennet, if you wish it."

"I do," Mary said, for they had much to discuss.

༄ Seventeen ༄

On the day Mr. Randall was to call at Longbourn, Mary found herself alone at the pianoforte, still pondering what she ought to do and say to her betrothed. Her fingers caressed the keys, but she hardly heard the resulting music.

How she wished she might discuss the matter with her mother or father, but surely they would only encourage her to hold her peace and marry Mr. Randall as planned. That was the sensible choice.

Mary longed to be sensible and rational, but she must discover the truth about the young woman. Though many wives seemed to coexist quite peacefully with a philandering husband, Mary knew herself well enough to be aware that she would not. Marrying a gentleman who loved another—whose eyes were ever focused on another—would be an unendurable fate. The town would pity her, and in her own household, she would be all but invisible. No one, not even her husband, would look upon her.

Though she had never contemplated the prospect of love, she must do so now. If Mr. Randall could not love Mary, then, at the very least, he must not give his heart to another woman. Mary could not bear knowing that with each look at her—his wife—he would be wishing another woman sat in her place.

Even if it cost everything, Mary would not allow that to happen.

She winced. She might very well lose her reputation and her place in society. As she once said of her sister Lydia, "Loss of virtue in a female is irretrievable—that one false step involves her in endless ruin—that her reputation is no less brittle than it is beautiful, and that she cannot be too much guarded in her behavior toward the undeserving of the other sex."

What a dreadful coincidence that her own moralization now applied to her.

A knock sounded at the door, and she knew Mr. Randall had arrived.

Mary's heart began to race. She must go destroy her brittle reputation.

∽◆◆ ◆◆∾

The best place to destroy one's reputation is in the beauty of God's creation. Before Mr. Randall could enter Longbourn, Mary suggested a walk. She had no patience for her mother's enthusiasm today. She must conduct her business and be done with it.

But how ought one begin such a conversation? Mary was well aware that there must be some technique for lessening the impact of sensitive topics, but she could not call it to mind.

Flustered, she stopped mid-stride and turned abruptly to Mr. Randall.

"Though I know it is utterly uncouth, I must speak plainly with you, Mr. Randall, and I wish that you would return the favor by answering with candor."

Mr. Randall tilted his blond head to the side, studying her with a fearful intensity.

"Yes," he said. "I believe we ought to be able to speak openly now that we are finally alone."

"Come," she said, leading him farther into the garden and away from the house. "Let us go where we might not be overheard."

Together, they settled upon a weathered stone bench on the fringes of the garden.

"Why did you propose to me, Mr. Randall?" Mary began, not bothering with pleasantries. "We were hardly acquainted before your letter."

Mr. Randall appeared unsurprised by her topic and answered immediately. "I suppose I proposed for the same reason that you accepted: it was what ought to be done."

Mary's stomach revolted at the very idea, but she nodded at Mr. Randall, grateful for his honest response. She was determined to reply with equal forthrightness. "We are doing our duty to our families. I am relieving my parents of the last daughter in their care."

"And I am gaining the money necessary to return Ashworth to rights." He inclined his head to her. "And we both acquire a pleasant companion."

Mary scowled but quickly schooled her features into neutrality. Mr. Randall truly was a kind gentleman, but she wanted more than a "pleasant companion."

"Forgive me, but I must ask—is there another of your acquaintance whom you might have married if your circumstances had been altered?"

Mr. Randall blanched and looked away. Mary interpreted that as confirmation and was preparing to probe deeper into the situation when he surprised her by saying, "I intended to ask the very same question of you."

Mary's eyes widened, and she gaped at the side of his head.

"I do not take your meaning, sir," she admitted, feeling panic rise in her throat. "Do you mean to accuse me of—"

"No, no," Mr. Randall said earnestly, turning toward her again. "Please do not believe me to be making these statements as accusations. I assume you did not mean to accuse me of wrongdoing."

"Certainly not," Mary replied. "I do not care to engage in dramatic accusations."

"Good."

Their gaze broke, and Mary found herself studying the toes of Mr. Randall's boots. Birdsong filled the silence for long minutes while they both gathered their courage.

Finally, Mary spoke, her voice slow and careful. "I merely wanted to ascertain whether this marriage contract was drawn too hastily."

She dared not look at him. Had she incited his ire? Had she insulted him? Would he now rail at her?

At length, Mr. Randall's voice came, also careful and steady through the soft sounds of the garden. "And perhaps the match was made against the wills of those it involved directly."

"Yes," Mary agreed, chancing a look at his face.

She discovered Mr. Randall to be watching her with neither anger nor sorrow in his expression. He leaned forward and took her hand in his.

"Tell me, Miss Bennet. Do you wish to marry me?"

Mary felt heat in her cheeks, but she kept her eyes steady on his. The irony of the picture they presented was not lost on her. Anyone observing them from the house would no doubt see a young couple very much in love, but the reality was quite the contrary.

Mary could not answer his question without first asking one of her own.

"Tell *me*, Mr. Randall. Is your heart engaged elsewhere?"

He hesitated, and Mary was quick to reassure him. "Never fear that you will injure me, for I am made of sturdier stuff than most imagine. You shall not hurt me unless you speak a falsehood. So please, speak plainly."

"I do love another," he admitted slowly.

"The young lady with whom I observed you at the ball?"

Mr. Randall nodded, and, with pleading eyes, he poured forth the entire story. "Miss Latimer is the daughter of my father's steward. We have known each other since we were children, and I have loved her nearly as long. Alas, my father will not hear of any union between us. He assures me that Ashworth will fall to ruin if I marry a woman with no dowry or inheritance, and I am responsible for the livelihoods of so many who inhabit the estate. And yet...."

Here, Mr. Randall's voice trailed into silence.

"You desire to marry Miss Latimer," Mary finished for him. "And she wishes the same."

"Yes. In fact, Miss Latimer and I had been considering an elopement. My father must have gotten wind of it, and when the news of your dowry reached us, well, he insisted that I must make you an offer."

Mary did not know how to feel. She had known that Mr. Darcy's money had been the inducement for his proposal, but hearing it said aloud quite battered her spirit.

When she did not respond immediately, Mr. Randall continued. "I gather that you find yourself in similar a circumstance: you also love another of whom your parents disapprove."

Mary swallowed and began to fumble with her skirt.

"I cannot admit to such a thing," Mary said. She sounded uncertain even to her own ears.

"Can you not?" Mr. Randall asked. "I observed you dancing with that tall gentleman. Mr. Hardcastle, I believe."

"Yes, we danced, though it was hardly improper," she said defensively. "A dance alone can signify very little."

"Or it can signify a great deal. I saw how he looked at you, Miss Bennet, and how you looked at him in return."

"How I looked at him?" Mary sputtered. "I looked upon him in no special manner. I can assure you that I have never once felt any symptoms of love. I do not think myself capable of it."

Mr. Randall leaned back, studying her face.

"Can you not?" he asked again. "Perhaps you are unaware of the 'symptoms of love' as you call them. Consider your time with Mr. Hardcastle. Have you not felt a certain quickening of your heart? A heating of your skin as if his gaze alone could set you aflame? A flutter in your midsection?"

Mary looked away, willing her face not to flush.

She had experienced those very sensations with Mr. Hardcastle. Was *that* love? She could hardly believe it to be true. Mary Bennet did not suffer love for Mr. Hardcastle. She felt an absurd attraction and nothing more.

"The symptoms you describe could be signs of bilious fever," she said flatly.

Mr. Randall laughed lightly. "I understand you, Miss Bennet. You do not wish to make your admission of feelings to anyone but the gentleman in question."

Mary shook her head in protest, fully prepared to rebuke him, but he continued. "Now, what shall we do about our situation?"

She chose her next words carefully. "It would be disingenuous indeed for us to marry," she finally said, "under conditions such as these."

"No, indeed, but my father will certainly object if I were to attempt to marry Miss Latimer."

"Because of your financial situation?" Mary surmised. Then, an idea struck her, and she gave voice to her thoughts. "Are you certain of the peril of your estate? Surely you have verified his assertion by checking the accounts."

Mr. Randall hung his head.

"You have not verified your estate's finances?" she asked incredulously. "Then it is possible that your father is manipulating you with a half-truth. Does your estate require additional money, or is he merely using it as an excuse to prevent your elopement with Miss Latimer? Would he do such a thing?"

"I had never considered such a possibility." Mr. Randall's eyes lit up. "Why, it might very well be true. I have seen no evidence of monetary retrenching on my father's part. The estate runs as it always has. Our table never lacks meat. We have no creditors. I must appeal to Mr. Latimer for the accounts and go over them myself."

Mary frowned. "Would not Miss Latimer be aware of the estate's finances? She is the daughter of your steward."

"Certainly not! Mr. Latimer is a master of discretion. He would never share our situation with his daughter, and moreover, he knows nothing of our relationship. No, Mr. Latimer would have no ulterior motivations."

He looked into the distance and scratched his chin thoughtfully.

"Regardless of what you discover, Mr. Randall," Mary said, drawing his attention from the horizon, "I have not the least wish of marrying you now."

"No, I suppose you cannot marry me any more than I could marry you now that I have clarified my own feelings for Miss Latimer. Were it not for my father, I would have married her already. You and I must break our engagement."

"But, sir, the papers have already been signed," she reminded him. "My fortune is legally entwined with yours."

"You have nothing to fear from me on that score," Mr. Randall assured her. "If my newfound suspicions are correct, and my father is exaggerating the depth of our need, then you have nothing to fear from him either."

Then, Mr. Randall leapt from the bench and promptly dropped to one knee before her. "We may not marry after all!"

Mary smiled at him, again pondering the oddness of the moment and fearing what might come next.

"Our engagement has been made public," she warned. "Ending it now would constitute a violent break with convention."

His face fell.

"You are right. It is wholly unacceptable for an honorable gentleman to withdraw an offer of marriage." He paused and looked at her with abject hope. "I may not do such a thing, but a lady may sever an engagement...."

"If she is strong enough to endure the label of 'jilt' and the ensuing ridicule," Mary supplied.

"Oh dear," he said, frowning. "You may not break our engagement without a great deal of censure. What are we to do?"

In that moment, Mary made her decision. "I am strong enough, Mr. Randall, provided that you agree not to sue for breach of promise."

He beamed at her and ran a hand through his blond curls.

"I have no wish to waste time dealing with legalities. I will take no legal action against you," he vowed again. Then, he paused to kiss her knuckles. "There! It is decided. Our engagement is broken!"

Though truly relieved, Mary could not share his enthusiasm, for as the woman, she knew she must face certain ridicule.

৩৫ Eighteen ৩৫

"Mr. Bennet! Mr. Bennet!" Mrs. Bennet shrieked and dashed toward his private chamber, arms waving wildly.

Feeling as if she headed to her own execution, Mary pressed her lips together and followed along behind her mother.

Mrs. Bennet flung herself through Mr. Bennet's door and shouted, "We are all ruined!"

"Again?" Mr. Bennet asked without rising from his chair. He did, however, put down his book and regard Mary thoughtfully. "What terrible tragedy has befallen us now?"

"Mary says she has called off her engagement to Mr. Randall!"

Mr. Bennet's eyebrows raised. "Did you do such a thing?"

Mary met his gaze steadily. "Yes, Papa, I did call off my engagement to Mr. Randall."

Mrs. Bennet fanned her face and then threw herself into a chair.

"Jilt! She will be forever known as a jilt!" she cried. "She shall never marry now! And the gossip! My poor nerves shall not survive it!"

Mr. Bennet rolled his eyes and called for Hill while Mrs. Bennet continued her theatrics.

When the housekeeper arrived a moment later, he said, "Please take Mrs. Bennet to her chamber, and see that she has whatever is required to calm her."

Hill hefted the wailing Mrs. Bennet from her chair and nearly carried her out of the room.

"I need pastries—at least a dozen fresh pastries—for only that will console me after what Mary has done!"

Their voices disappeared, and the house fell silent.

Mary looked at her father.

"What precipitated this turn of events?" Mr. Bennet asked, his voice gentle.

"Mr. Randall and I discovered that certain members of our families desired our marriage far more than we did ourselves."

"I see," Mr. Bennet said.

"He has agreed not to sue for breach of promise, and I am willing to face the consequences that must fall upon me." Mary paused and lowered her head, still regarding her father from beneath her lashes. "Are you very angry with me?"

"Angry?" Mr. Bennet repeated, his tone verging on amusement. "No, I am not angry at you, Mary."

"But how is that possible? I have brought shame to the door of Longbourn. I deserve your censure."

Mr. Bennet stood, rounded the desk, and stopped beside his daughter. Kneeling, he placed a hand on her arm.

"Look at me, Daughter."

Mary did so, and found him to be regarding her earnestly.

"When first you sat in this chair all those weeks ago, I told you to choose wisely whom you would wed."

Mary nodded, remembering his words clearly.

"And when you last sat in this chair—with Mr. Hardcastle present—I signed the contracts upon your direction."

Mary nodded again.

"I have always allowed my daughters to choose their husbands freely, have I not?" he asked. "Even foolish Lydia selected her mate in her own way. As did Jane and Lizzie, though they were wiser about it."

"I thought I was being wise," Mary admitted. "I believed it best to follow Mama's guidance and engage myself to a gentleman who would provide me with a home and security. You too advised to me make the best possible use of Mr. Darcy's gift."

"I did say that Mr. Darcy's gift should be used responsibly but according to your choice."

"I believed myself to be making a good choice. I did not allow myself to be influenced by emotion. Is it not said that every impulse of feeling should be guided by reason? That is what I have read. I was attempting to follow that exhortation."

"My dear," Mr. Bennet said, "you have an impressive breadth of knowledge, but blindly following the words of any book is not true wisdom. You must first test those words; discover for yourself what is true. That is wisdom."

Mary scrunched her nose. "I do not know how to make such a judgment."

"That is not true, for you have made the first sound judgment just today. You have called off your engagement for sober, wise reasons. You have seen fit to minimize the consequences and accept what remains. I am proud of you, and I shall contact Mr. Philips to terminate the marriage contract."

Mary managed a small smile. If her father was right, and she had minimized the risk, then perhaps she might manage to survive this humiliation yet.

৩৫ Nineteen ৯৯৵

What followed was so great a disaster that not even a bakery full of pastries could mollify Mrs. Bennet.

Seven days had not passed when Mr. John Randall arrived at Longbourn and stormed into Mr. Bennet's private chamber.

Mary, who had glimpsed his arrival from an upstairs window, hurried below stairs to listen at the door. She soon discovered that she had not been required to stand so close, for everyone in the household could hear Mr. Randall's bellows of indignation.

His imprecations burned Mary's ears, but she felt true physical pain when she heard him shout, "An engagement contract is made between families as well as between two individuals, and your family has not upheld its portion of the bargain! There must be legal implications."

Upon those words, the door flung open, nearly knocking Mary in the head. She shuffled back, avoiding the blow, but when Mr. Randall glowered at her, she did not shrink back.

"Get out of my way," Mr. Randall said through clenched teeth, "you stupid chit."

Mary's chest puffed with indignation, and she did not shift herself from his path. "I was given to understand that Mr. Randall would not sue."

"My son's opinion in the matter does not signify," he spat. "What you have done, Miss Bennet, in spurning my son is to ruin your entire family."

Mary had no retort, for the elder Mr. Randall spoke the truth. If he sued for Mary's dowry, she would lose ten thousand pounds. That was a vast amount of money.

Mary remained solidly where she stood while Mr. Randall sidestepped her and then stomped out of the house. Mr. Bennet appeared beside her.

"Oh, Mary," he said, looping an arm around her shoulders. "Surely, there is no way one family can have the good fortune of extricating itself from two such events. First Lydia and now this."

His voice held a mixture of concern and amusement that caused Mary to look at him sharply.

"Even this has not angered you, Papa?"

"Well, I wish you had spared me the trouble of it all." He gave her shoulder another squeeze. "It is very likely that Mr. Darcy's dowry will be lost. Your brother-in-law will certainly be displeased at the careless use of his funds."

Mary felt tears gathering in her eyes. Despite her father's light treatment of the situation, a great deal more was now lost to her than ten thousand pounds and Mr. Darcy's approval.

She had forfeited her potential for happiness.

And so much more.

While Mr. Randall would be free to marry Miss Latimer, Mary would never wed.

And while the elder Mr. Randall would yet receive Mr. Darcy's money, Mary would be poor for the rest of her days. Worse, she would forever be a disappointment, shuffled off to one of her sisters' homes to be forgotten.

In fact, the ostracism had already begun. Since the news broke, Mary had received no invitations to social events, and few people paid morning calls to Longbourn, leaving Mrs. Bennet quite put out.

After the day when Mr. Randall stormed out, Mary spent a great many hours at Mrs. Bennet's bedside, where she endured nearly constant blame for the manner in which the Bennet family had been brought low.

Even now, she sat in a small wooden chair in her mother's chamber and listened to another tirade.

"I do not understand it, Hill," Mrs. Bennet said, stuffing a pastry in her mouth. "How could Mr. Bennet allow such foolishness? Mary must not break her engagement to Mr. Randall! And yet Mr. Bennet approves the decision and even facilitates it? How could he allow it?"

Having served in the Bennet household for many years, Hill knew better than to offer much by way of response.

After a few blissful moments of quiet, Mrs. Bennet perceived that Hill would not commiserate with her and, thus, continued her tirade.

"Whatever shall we do with Mary now? No gentleman wanted her before the dowry, and none will have her after this business with the Randalls! What will become of her after Mr. Bennet is gone, and the house has passed on to Mr. Collins? I shall, of course, go to Pemberley, but I do not believe Mr. Darcy will have Mary after her careless treatment of his gift. Besides, Kitty is already in their care."

Again, Hill wisely remained silent, but she offered Mary a smile.

"She may be welcome with Jane, but Mr. Bingley is not half so rich as Mr. Darcy. And Lydia and Mr. Wickham travel far too often to take her."

Mary fidgeted in her chair. Mrs. Bennet may not always choose her words kindly, but she certainly managed to express the truth. In this instance, her mother happened to be alarmingly accurate in her assessment of Mary's situation.

Her stomach churned as she pictured the life that lay before her. She would live with her parents until her father expired. Then, Mary would not truly be welcome anywhere. She would forever be a burden upon one of her sisters.

A tear slid down her cheek, but she brushed it away before her mother marked it. She could not allow her mother to believe she regretted her decision, for she did not.

But she also did not relish the future she had created for herself.

The loss of Mr. Darcy's money ensured that she would not be invited to Pemberley to enjoy the comforts of its library. Living with Lydia was out of the question, and Jane's house, though comfortable, would hold little to amuse her. Mr. Bingley was a kind gentleman, but he was not a great reader and had no library.

Mary dropped her head into her hands. She would never have the chance of happiness.

In the background, her mother shrieked, "But the money, Hill! It would all be bearable if she had not lost it to those dreadful Randalls."

Again, Mrs. Bennet's thoughtless words tore at Mary's heart. Her mother was right. The burden of a broken engagement was far easier when it was not yoked to the loss of ten thousand pounds.

As her father had said, "For good or ill, money buys marriage, which brings security."

It was ever about the money. Everything started and ended with it.

Gaining the money had sent Mary's life into chaos, but she always believed she would emerge from the chaos a happier woman. But losing the money? Losing it meant far worse. She could never emerge from the chaos, and she would be neither happy nor secure.

Money was both the problem and the solution to her problem.

In that moment, with echoes of her mother's voice tearing through her very being, Mary realized what she must do.

❦ Twenty ❧

Leaping from her seat, Mary tore down the stairs and to the door, barely pausing to gather her pelisse and bonnet. In her dash from the house, she never considered calling for the carriage. Though she despised walking, she hurried on foot all the way to Meryton and her uncle's law firm.

Upon entering the office, she discovered Mr. Hardcastle alone. Abruptly, he unfolded himself from behind a cluttered worktable and studied her with wide eyes. He had shed himself of his coat, which was most inappropriate when receiving a female caller, but Mary could not muster any sentiment on the matter. Not one quote on proper decorum came to her mind.

She was already labeled a jilt; she might as well also be seen with a man *en dishabille*.

"Miss Bennet!" he exclaimed.

"Mr. Hardcastle," Mary said, hiding her inexplicable pleasure at having found him in this state.

"You have come." His words sounded almost as if he were stating a fact aloud so that he himself might better comprehend it. Quickly, he added, "To see your uncle, of course. But he is not here."

"Yes. No," Mary said, clutching the fabric of her pelisse. "I am here to see you."

She had hoped to find him alone, for she had no wish to wound her uncle by openly doubting his legal prowess.

Mr. Hardcastle waited.

"I have come to take you up on your offer of aid."

"I see," he said, jostling a precarious stack of papers as he rounded the table and drew nearer.

"I am certain that you are aware of my situation."

He nodded, his face carefully blank. "I am sorry to say that the news of what has transpired between your family and the Randalls of Ashworth is rather well known. My sister and your uncle have talked of nothing else for days."

Mary's gaze dropped to the floor. "Although I am not surprised, I am very sorry to hear that. You must be rather tired of hearing my troubles, and yet I bring them to your door."

They said nothing for long moments, and Mary contemplated the wisdom of what she was preparing to do.

"Shall we sit?" Mr. Hardcastle asked, interrupting her silent deliberation.

"No, no," Mary said, looking at him again. "I have come for a purpose."

"Yes, you mentioned that," he said, standing idly before her. "What may I do to help you?"

"I am given to understand that there can be legitimate reasons a contract might be voided. Perhaps Mr. Randall's lawyer committed some error in the marriage settlement."

Mr. Hardcastle raised an eyebrow and gave her a guilty grin.

"Do not ask me why," he said carefully, extending his arm to her, "but I happen to have acquired a copy of the contract from your uncle's desk. I have spent the balance of the day searching it for just such a flaw."

Mary's hand rose to her heart, and she made no move to take his arm. He had procured the contract and was already in the process of rendering aid. That could mean only that Mr. Hardcastle had thought of her, not as gossip fodder, but as a young lady worthy of gentlemanly assistance.

Not only had Mr. Hardcastle seen her, but he also had deemed her worthy, despite her mistakes.

The same odd sensation fluttered through her, but thanks to her conversation with Mr. Randall, she surmised its origin.

Mary Bennet loved Mr. Hardcastle.

But her realization had come far too late.

Still, she could not prevent herself the pleasure of raising her hand to his arm, allowing her fingertips to brush over the fabric of his shirt. His opposite hand covered hers, and her breath caught in her throat at the naked caress. His fingers were stained with ink, but they were warm and comforting.

She dared to look at his eyes and found them steadily regarding her.

"Come," he said softly. "Let us see if we might rectify this."

Mr. Hardcastle settled Mary in a hard wooden chair at his worktable and procured another for himself.

Spreading the papers before her, he said, "I have searched for all the usual errors, but I could spot nothing. Perhaps you will be able to see some aspect I overlooked."

The ink blurred before her eyes. Mr. Hardcastle did her the honor of honesty in telling her that she had only a small chance for success. She knew little about the legal profession and even less about marriage contracts, but still, she must try. Her hand trembled as she adjusted the papers.

She read the contract once.

As he had predicted, Mary could see nothing in the verbiage that might extricate her family from the loss of Mr. Darcy's generous bestowal.

As if reading her thoughts, Mr. Hardcastle said, "My sister explained the origins of your dowry."

Mary turned emotional eyes upon him and hoped desperately not to find pity in his expression.

"Do not be angry with Penelope," he implored. "It was her worry for your future that motivated her, and nothing else. She knows what it is to be without means."

Mary felt a strange bolt of jealous anger surge in her.

"Miss Hardcastle is a beauty," she said, "and a beauty is loved wherever she goes. A rich gentleman will one day see her and desire her. The same cannot be said of me."

Then, she stood and began to pace behind the desk. "I must apologize," she added. "My emotions are far too close to the surface, I fear."

Mr. Hardcastle did not turn from the papers. "It is nothing, Miss Bennet," he murmured.

"I do not wish you to believe me a slave to mammon," Mary said, faltering slightly. She gestured at the paper. "It is not money that compels me to seek faults in that contract. I have never hoped for riches."

Mr. Hardcastle adjusted so that he now faced Mary as she continued on her path back and forth across the room.

"Why then?" he asked. "To please your family?"

"I am not convinced that my mother can be truly pleased by any eventuality," Mary muttered.

She stopped pacing, but did not turn toward him. She could not quite bring herself to speak the truth yet. She had only just become acquainted with her heart. She could not divulge its contents so soon.

"I must study this document," she whispered instead as she returned to the table and focused on the papers.

Mr. Hardcastle remained silent beside her.

An hour passed.

Then another.

Mr. Hardcastle came and went, and still, Mary read.

At some point, a teacup appeared beside her, and she drank without realizing she had done so.

Mary's head ached, and her heart had plummeted to the depths of despair. Why had she ever believed that she might find some hidden flaw in the marriage settlement? Mr. Randall's attorney was thorough in his work. Otherwise, her uncle would never have advised her father to sign. Mr. Hardcastle had also searched the words and found nothing.

There was no hope to be had for Mary.

She plunked her elbows on the table and dropped her face into her hands. Without a thought to the propriety of her deportment, she moaned, "Why, oh, why did I ever accept him?"

"Yes, why did you?" Mr. Hardcastle asked, his voice bland as he appeared in the chair beside her.

"Oh! I do not know," Mary wailed, sounding frighteningly like her mother. Upon that unpleasant realization, she paused to compose herself. After a moment's thought, she found she had reconsidered. "That is a falsehood. I do know."

She looked at Mr. Hardcastle's curious expression and decided that no matter what she confessed, no further damage could be done.

"Since my sisters all left home, I have come to realize that I have wasted my life striving for accomplishments that no one truly appreciates. I have spent hours at the pianoforte, only to discover that my voice can never accompany me. I have read, only to find that people believe I moralize when I discuss the books I love. For once, I wanted to do something that would create pride in the gazes of my mother and father."

"And that is all?" he asked.

Mary regarded him more closely. It appeared that her response was of utmost importance to him. She remained silent. Was he asking if she had loved Mr. Randall?

Surely, he must know that her acceptance of Mr. George Randall had nothing to do with sentiment. Mary Bennet had never been in love.

Until now.

Until she had met Mr. Hardcastle.

But it was too late. She could not expect him to take her now that she was thus soiled.

"Also, because," Mary added lamely, "the library at Ashford is said to be well stocked."

Her whisper died away into silence, and the warmth of the room seemed to tuck itself around them. Mary's heart thumped wildly in her chest at the tender expression on Mr. Hardcastle's face.

But he did not reach for her.

How could he? She had ruined herself. No honorable gentleman would deign to romance a penniless jilt.

She stood again, her legs protesting after having remained so long in one attitude.

"I have been moral and good, and now I am poor and a jilt. Perhaps I should have listened to my uncle and avoided aligning myself with a gentleman of Gallic descent."

Her head snapped up.

"Gallic descent," she repeated.

"I did not know Randall was a French name," Mr. Hardcastle said, confused.

"No, it is not. But his Christian name…Mr. Hardcastle, that is it! His name!"

"What? You are speaking in riddles."

Mary took a steadying breath.

"Gossips in town often recount a tale about the late Mrs. Randall. She insisted her firstborn be given her family name. A name she shared with Napoleon Bonaparte's mistress, who later became his wife." She frowned in thought, but the name refused to make itself known. "I cannot recall the name she gave him, but Mr. Randall despised it and began calling him George after his wife's death."

"George is not his given name?" Mr. Hardcastle asked, scrabbling for the papers.

"No," Mary said, wracking her brain. "It is…it is…Beauharnais."

She threw herself toward the table, hunching over as they both scoured the documents.

"Here it is!" he cried, turning his head so that he faced Mary. "George Randall to marry Mary Bennet, etcetera. They have not used his proper given name."

Their faces were close as she beamed at him.

Mr. Hardcastle's eyes searched hers, and the room suddenly felt too small and far too intimate.

Mary licked her lips, and his gaze dropped to her mouth.

She straightened and cleared her throat. "Is that sufficient grounds for nullifying the document?"

Mr. Hardcastle also cleared his throat and stood. "First, we must verify his true given name. The parish church ought to have a record of his baptism."

"Yes!" Mary said. "I am certain his mother remained alive long enough to insist upon its use when he was christened."

Mr. Hardcastle gave a sharp nod of confirmation. "Then, once we have the proof, Mr. Philips will be able to argue for the voiding of the contract."

"Oh, thank heavens," Mary breathed.

Suddenly, her heart felt both lighter and heavier. She and Mr. Hardcastle may have managed to salvage Mr. Darcy's gift, but all the money in England would do her little good in securing a husband now that she was deemed a jilt. However, its return may allow her one day to make Pemberley her home. There, she would be forgotten just as much as she would at any other place, but at least she would have the comfort of books.

Mary turned to Mr. Hardcastle and gave him a watery smile. "I must offer you my deepest gratitude for your help, sir."

He stood, briefly met her eyes, and then looked away almost bashfully. "You owe me no thanks, Miss Bennet. I desired to aid you, and I shall continue to do so by applying to the rector."

The air in the room thickened, and Mary felt as if breathing had suddenly become an unfamiliar act. Mr. Hardcastle stepped closer.

"Miss Bennet," he whispered. "I—"

"I must go," she said quickly, unable to bear what he might say. "I must tell my parents the happy news."

She pivoted on her heel, nearly knocking over Mr. Hardcastle's vacated chair in the process, and stumbled out of her uncle's law office.

Behind her, she heard a rough whisper.

"Mary…."

Not ready to face her own heart, Mary fled.

∞ Twenty-one ∞

Upon the dissolution of the marriage settlement, Mr. John Randall arrived promptly at Longbourn to pay a pleasant call upon Mr. Bennet.

Having expected his arrival, Mary greeted him at the door with an innocent grin.

"Do come in, Mr. Randall," she said, her voice laced with graciousness. "I see that you have come for a morning call. Shall I request tea?"

Mr. Randall's face purpled, and he sputtered wordlessly at her.

Mary wondered when she had become so brazen. For years, she had managed no thoughts that had not first been recorded in books, but now, she spoke her own mind. Perhaps the characteristic had not been as absent from her as she had believed, but dormant, awaiting its moment to awaken.

"Where is your father?" he demanded, pushing past her and stomping down the hall. "I will speak with him."

She followed, calling after him, "If you will wait here, I shall summon him."

Mr. Randall pounded at her father's door and then opened it himself.

Mr. Bennet stood, but his face registered no surprise.

Mary stepped past the angry man. "Papa, Mr. Randall has come to see you, and he refuses to wait at the door."

"Well," Mr. Bennet said, his voice full of irony, "then he must come in."

By this time, Mr. Randall's knees already brushed against the front of Mr. Bennet's desk.

"You are no kind of a gentleman!" he shouted.

Mr. Bennet returned to his seat and languidly regarded the intruder, who now glowered at him.

"And you are obviously unaware of the rules of propriety that discourage a guest from barging into a gentleman's private chamber and interrupting his solitude."

Mr. Randall clenched his fists and slammed them onto the desk.

"Besides which," Mr. Bennet continued, "you have come to rail at me for discovering the flaw in the marriage contract—"

"It was no flaw! His name is George!"

"Not according to the law," Mr. Bennet said gleefully. "Moreover, you have come to this door in error, sir. I did not discover the flaw. The credit goes to my daughter alone."

Mr. Randall spun and glared at Mary.

Behind him, Mr. Bennet smiled at his daughter and said, "You have been out-maneuvered by a female."

Mr. Bennet rose, turning his back on his guest and facing Mary instead.

"I wish I could say that I was unsurprised by her actions," he said, still addressing his guest but looking only at Mary. "I believed her to be as foolish as a young girl could be, and her engagement to your son seemed to confirm that belief."

Mr. Randall made a guttural sound in his throat as Mr. Bennet continued.

"But her methods of extricating herself from what was so clearly an endeavor to gain her money were far beyond what I expected."

Awestruck, Mary stared at her father as tears filled her eyes. Mr. Bennet had always preferred Lizzie and had reserved such compliments for her alone. He had never spoken to Mary with such candor and respect.

A tear slid down her cheek, and her regret slid away with it. She would engage herself to Mr. Randall a thousand times over if it meant this one moment with her father.

"Very fine words, Mr. Bennet," Mr. Randall managed to say. "But her cleverness will be to her detriment."

"Oh?" her father asked. "How so?"

"Polite society will never receive her, and no gentleman of means—or lack thereof—will have her now."

"That may indeed be true," Mr. Bennet agreed in an affable tone, "but I no longer doubt that Mary shall be able to endure whatever her future holds."

✆ Twenty-two ✆

"Why does this dress refuse to button?" Mrs. Bennet demanded of Hill, who stood behind her mistress and attempted to stuff her completely inside the garment.

Under her breath, Hill muttered something about "dozens of pastries," and Mary smiled at her.

Life at Longbourn had returned to normal; however, Meryton society had not yet welcomed the Bennets back into the fold.

Mr. Bennet assured Mary that it was only a matter of time. They had suffered little after Lydia's scandal with Mr. Wickham. Soon, Meryton would forget about Mary and Mr. Randall as well.

In the meantime, Mrs. Philips called upon them, often bringing with her Miss Hardcastle and news from Meryton.

On one such call, the two ladies were accompanied by a single gentleman: Mr. Hardcastle.

Mary managed a polite curtsy to him, but her heart leapt within her chest at the sight of him.

"Oh, Mr. Hardcastle," Mrs. Bennet said, waving him toward the tall-backed chair beside the window. "Do sit down. You honor us with your presence. You are the first gentleman to darken this door since...well...since—"

"It was good of you to come," Mary supplied when her mother could not find a way out of her oratorical dilemma. "Would you care to sit?"

"No, I have no wish to sit," he said bluntly. "I hoped you might take a turn in the garden with me, Miss Bennet."

Mary's face flushed, and she appealed to her mother for permission.

Mrs. Bennet's eyebrows met her hairline. "Oh yes! Do take our Mary wherever you wish, Mr. Hardcastle. Oh! Oh!" She turned to Mrs. Philips. "He wants to take a turn with her...*in the garden*. All hope is not lost!"

Mr. Hardcastle smiled at her mother's obvious display and offered his arm. Mary took it, grateful to be free of the room.

"I must apologize for my mother," Mary said when she and Mr. Hardcastle were safely out of doors. "My family, it seems, often struggles to make appropriate conversation. Unfortunately, I seem to have inherited the trait."

"I have always understood you, Miss Bennet," Mr. Hardcastle said. His boots crunched softly on the garden path as they walked. "And I have always fancied that you understood me as well. Even when we spoke mostly in quotations."

Mary lowered her eyes, watching her own steps slow, and shook her head.

"I have hardly understood myself until recently," she admitted. "I have made so many mistakes that I do not wish to make another by assuming anything about you."

Mr. Hardcastle halted, causing Mary to stop abruptly a step later. She turned to face him but could not manage to meet his eyes.

"Then, let me tell you bluntly," he said, using his index finger to tip her chin up and then lingering at her jawline. "I am in love with you and wish to marry you."

His declaration held no poetry at all, and Mary could not but approve of his forthright honesty, for now she knew without a doubt that Mr. Hardcastle loved her. Her face lit with joy, and happiness robbed her of words. In lieu of speech, she pressed her palm to his cheek. Her eyes slid shut as she savored her moment of pure feeling.

"Say something, Mary," Mr. Hardcastle said, his voice hoarse.

Mary opened her eyes and saw that Mr. Hardcastle, whose bearing was usually so confident and certain, appeared utterly unsure.

"My heart," she finally managed to whisper, "is too full of feeling to allow my mind to compose words."

"Is it?" Mr. Hardcastle asked in a gentle tone. "What feelings?"

"Gratitude," Mary replied.

"Gratitude?" His face fell. "I am glad for it, but is that all? Is that the balance of your feelings toward me?"

"No," she whispered but could admit no more.

"Shall I tell you what *I* feel, Mary?"

Mary could only nod in response.

"I wish that I might seek your hand in marriage. I am painfully aware that I have nothing to offer a wife, especially one who brings with her a dowry. I thought I had no right to speak to you, but my sister encouraged me to give voice to my heart...even before your engagement."

"I am not engaged any longer," Mary reminded him.

"Still, I do not see why you would consent to marry a penniless clerk from your uncle's law office. Your dowry means you might outrun the gossip in Hertfordshire and ensnare a landed gentleman with a name, a house, a library—"

"Stop," Mary whispered, blinking back tears. "I have no wish to leave Hertfordshire, for it is my home. Moreover, I have no desire to marry any gentleman whose only inducement to matrimony is a house or the grandest library I can imagine."

"No?" he asked softly.

"Perhaps all of Hertfordshire—nay, all of history—may believe that Mary Bennet obtained nothing higher than one of her uncle's clerks, but we shall know the truth."

"What truth is that?" Mr. Hardcastle asked, stepping closer and taking her hand in his.

"That though a union between us might not merit whispers of our exchange of pounds and land, we shall have something more valuable. We shall have the comfort of like minds. We comprehend each other, and we love each other, despite the faults that others may observe in us."

He regarded her with bright eyes.

"But I must caution you, sir," Mary said, her tone even more serious than before. "In making your proposal to me, you are aligning yourself with a known jilt. I am infamous, you know. Hertfordshire will always remember that I broke my engagement to an honorable suitor and that we outwitted his father. They will believe you the worst of gentlemen, saving my fortune only to abscond with it yourself."

Mr. Hardcastle shook his head violently, and his grip tightened on her hand. "Damn your dowry," he stated in a strangely factual matter, as if he had literally sent her money to eternal condemnation. "I have no wish for it. You shall have it all for pin money."

Mary could not help but feel relief at his offer, for she did not want money to be the impetus behind her marriage.

"I shall agree to such an offer only if you are aware of my intentions for its use," Mary said.

"What intentions?"

"I shall create a library for us, wherever we shall live. And we shall keep a carriage and some horses, for I despise walking."

Mr. Randall smiled and stepped closer, his face now only inches from hers. "You shall do with your dowry as you see fit, and I shall draw up the papers."

"And you shall use your true name?" Mary asked, feeling cheeky.

"Indeed, I shall," Mr. Hardcastle agreed, "for I am well aware that you would spot such a ploy and punish me."

Mary smiled at him, and his gaze dropped to her lips. In response, she lowered her lashes, feeling a rush of warmth and uncertainty.

Mary had never imagined what the embrace of a gentleman might feel like, so she had no expectations when Mr. Hardcastle bent, his arms circling her waist, and pulled her closer than propriety must allow. She had not anticipated the scent of him, the manner in which it overwhelmed her senses, or the feel of his cheek against her own.

She found herself to be clutching Mr. Hardcastle's lapels as her lips fell open in a small gasp.

Encouraged, Mr. Hardcastle groaned and pressed his lips to hers.

✺ Epilogue ✺

[Jane Austen] would, if asked, tell us many little particulars about the
subsequent career of some of her people.
In this traditionary way, we learned that…
Mary [Bennet] obtained nothing higher than one of her uncle Philip's
clerks,
and was content to be considered a star in the society of Meriton [sic].

—James Austen Leigh, *Memoir of Jane Austen*

✺ ✺

"Did I not tell you that Mr. Hardcastle was the proper gentleman for my Mary?" Mrs. Bennet asked Mrs. Philips.

Mrs. Philips nodded. "Indeed, you did, Sister. You have a talent for matchmaking."

From her place in her very own sitting room, Mary smiled wryly at her mother and aunt.

"Yes, Mama. You were right. Mr. Hardcastle is the proper gentleman for me."

Following their marriage, which did not devolve into a contractual dispute, Mr. and Mrs. Hardcastle had taken possession of a small house in Meryton. Miss Hardcastle, who remained in her brother's care, lived with them and kept house for Mary, who was far too busy compiling books for their library to trifle with meal planning and other household endeavors.

Mrs. Bennet and Mrs. Philips were frequent visitors to their home, always bringing with them the freshest gossip.

"You have heard the news about Mr. George Randall, have you not, Mary?" Mrs. Bennet asked.

Mary exchanged a quick glance with Miss Hardcastle, who sat beside her.

"No, indeed. You know I care nothing for gossip. 'Whoso keepeth his mouth and his tongue keepeth his soul from troubles,'" Mary said, deliberately choosing to use a quotation.

Mrs. Bennet's eyes narrowed. Mrs. Philips, however, intent on her gossip, remained ignorant of the exchange.

"Mr. George Randall has eloped with the daughter of his father's steward! Mr. John Randall is enraged, of course, but that is nothing new."

"When did this occur?" Mary asked, utterly unsurprised.

"Some days ago," Mrs. Philips said. "It is said that he will soon return with his new wife."

"I imagine the gossips are quite occupied with spreading rumors about what happened between us," Mary said.

"I am sorry to say it is so," Mrs. Philips replied. "First, they were content to make conjectures about the broken engagement. Now, they pass time by contemplating the reasons for your suspiciously sudden marriage to Mr. Hardcastle and Mr. Randall's equally sudden elopement."

Miss Hardcastle laughed merrily. "Yes, there must be some nefarious motive. Certainly, not love."

Still rather uncomfortable with her feelings, Mary did not reply. She cared little for gossip whether she heard it from her mother or her aunt, and she abhorred being its focus.

❧ ❧

Later that evening, she confronted Mr. Hardcastle with her discomfort. In response, he leaned back in his chair and gave her a quizzical look.

Mary pressed a fingertip to his lips and said, "A wise man does not remind his wife of her former preoccupation with seeking society's approval. Proverbs, I believe."

Mr. Hardcastle kissed her finger and then held it in his hands.

"I do not believe that is canonical," he replied, and then paused to consider her question. Finally, he proclaimed, "We must host a dinner party."

Mary frowned, sliding her hand from his grasp. "A dinner party? That is the most absurd thing I have heard all day, and I have been subject to my mother's detailed accounts of Meryton gossip!"

"Absurd? I hardly believe so," he said, giving her a devious look. "If the gossips enjoy their fiction so much, then let us shock them with some facts. Let us invite the principle players for a meal: your parents, Mr. and Mrs. Philips, Mr. and Mrs. George Randall, and every known gossip in the county. My sister can plan the evening, which will give her much pleasure. She does enjoy a spectacle."

"I do not see how such an event would quell the gossip about us at all."

"Oh, it shall not quell the gossip," he admitted, giving Mary another wicked grin. "If people enjoy creating melodrama where none exists, then let us help them along."

"You have gone mad," Mary declared. "You despise dinner parties and social spectacles, and yet you desire to parade about, creating gossip deliberately."

"Indeed, I do despise dinner parties, but I do so enjoy making fools of the foolish," he said. "And this is an exercise in honesty and forthrightness, two traits I greatly respect. I am suggesting that we meet our detractors head on and allow them to see the truth. Surely, there is no madness in that."

Mary mulled over the idea.

"They shall expect a scandal," she said at length. "But the Randalls and the Hardcastles shall behave charmingly to one another. It shall be a dull affair. The gossips will leave unsatisfied."

"Quite right, my dear, but people often see what they desire, not what actually exists. Let them interpret the evening to fit their own liking, and let us enjoy the fruits of their foolishness."

⚜

The Hardcastles' first dinner party became the county's most sought-after invitation. In the intervening weeks, distant acquaintances paid Mary morning calls, hoping to be extended an offer to join.

Everyone, it seemed, was eager to share a meal with Meryton's most infamous jilt, the gentleman whose heart she broke, and their new spouses.

Mary could have been offended that she had devolved into a mere curiosity, but after consideration, she realized that her husband had spoken true. Once an opinion is formed in a person's mind, it can be dismantled only through consistent action. Her words would never convince anyone of her innocence. She must not "protest too much."

Until the tide of opinion began to shift, Mary might as well make the most of her newfound infamy and solidify her place in society.

And so she plunged wholeheartedly into the escapade.

The dinner party was carried off with great success. Miss Hardcastle's meal was declared to be the most delicious ever served, and Mr. Hardcastle's sardonic commentary was recorded as the most humorous ever heard. After the meal,

Mary took the opportunity to play her longest, most intricate concerto, which was received with gracious applause and the player declared to be Meryton's finest musician.

And when at last the guests departed, and Miss Hardcastle had vanished above stairs, Mary found herself in the library with her husband. Books forgotten, he lay with his head in her lap.

"You see, my dear wife," he said, reaching up to cup her cheek in his palm, "you must never doubt me. People will recount the events of this evening for years to come."

"Yes, but what shall they say?" Mary wondered, enjoying her husband's touch.

"It hardly matters," said he, "for tonight, the clouds have parted, and Meryton sees you, Mary Hardcastle, for the star you have always been."

❧ ❧

✦ Acknowledgements ✦

I am most indebted to Jane Austen for her creation of the wonderful world and characters of *Pride and Prejudice*. My deepest thanks go to my editorial team—Jakki Leatherberry, Kelley Fuller Land, Octavia Becton, Marilyn Whiteley, and Bert Becton. As always, all mistakes in this text belong to me, but I will try to foist them off on someone else.

✦ ✦

✎ About the Author ✎

Jennifer Becton worked for more than twelve years in the traditional publishing industry as a freelance writer, editor, and proofreader. Upon discovering the possibilities of the expanding ebook market, she created Whiteley Press, LLC, an independent publishing house, and she has since published in two genres: historical fiction and thrillers. The Personages of *Pride and Prejudice* Collection includes *Charlotte Collins*, *Caroline Bingley*, "*Maria Lucas*," and Mary Bennet. *Absolute Liability*, *Death Benefits*, *At Fault*, and *Moral Hazard* are the first four volumes in the six-book Southern Fraud Thriller series.

Please join the Whiteley Press Launch List to be alerted when the next books in the Personages of *Pride & Prejudice* Collection and the Southern Fraud series are published. Also, check out the growing selection of Whiteley Press, LLC, audiobooks titles.

✎ ✎

Connect with Jennifer Online
Blog: http://www.bectonliterary.com

Facebook: http://www.facebook.com/JenniferBectonWriter

Twitter: http://twitter.com/JenniferBecton

Southern Fraud Thriller Series: http://www.jwbecton.com

Whiteley Press Launch List: http://eepurl.com/o-leX

✎ ✎

www.ingramcontent.com/pod-product-compliance
Lightning Source LLC
Chambersburg PA
CBHW020411150626
46554CB00013B/656